Murder at the Manor House

M*urder. Manor homes. Malfunctioning chandeliers.*

Hollywood starlets are supposed to be happily on set in sunny California and not trapped in drafty manor houses during ferocious snowstorms.

But after Cora Clarke's best friend and fellow actress elopes with an English earl, Cora visits England to help her friend brave the aristocratic disapproval of her new husband's family.

Unfortunately, the holiday turns nightmarish when a chandelier crashes down and kills somebody. When suspicion falls on her friend, Cora vows to figure out the identity of the murderer. After all, blizzards have a habit of preventing the police from arriving, and body counts have a dreadful habit of growing.

Prologue

Jabberist

December 1937

Lord Holt's elopement with American sensation Veronica James continues to rattle society's finest. The world may be distraught at having lost a prized actress, but English aristocrats are appalled at having gained one.

Hollywood's go-to actress for vamps is officially a countess.

The Duke and Duchess of Hawley are reportedly furious at their son's elopement. We are glad we will be nowhere near the duke's estate in Yorkshire, where Lord Holt and his new, utterly inappropriate bride, plan to spend the holidays.

Chapter One

Twig breakage rarely seemed intriguing, but perhaps because Veronica's housekeeper was taking a long time to answer the door, or perhaps because Cora needed distraction from her day, she glanced toward the sound.

A man was hiding beneath the hibiscus.

The bushes poked the man's suit, and he held his head at an odd angle as he directed the black-and-chrome camera in his hand at her. The lavender blossoms seemed incongruous against his dark attire. This might be Bel Air, the center of everything luxurious, but Cora doubted the ground was comfortable.

Unease shot through her, and she considered screaming.

But then, likely he might find her screaming amusing.

Or lucrative.

Unfortunately, she wasn't confident in her ability to open her mouth to the width required for a properly audible scream *and* retain some semblance of refinement. The camera in the man's hand made the latter consideration necessary.

Throwing her handbag at him was tempting, though it might compel him to rifle through it. He didn't need to learn it didn't contain any money.

Cora turned around, caught the attention of the guard who'd let her through the imposing wrought-iron gates of Veronica's mansion, and yelled, "There's an intruder!"

She waited for him to rush toward her, baton in hand.

Instead, the guard smiled back and waved amiably.

Hmph.

Cora cursed Veronica for acquiring the largest lot in Bel Air.

The ocean was similarly unhelpful. Though the manner in which the foamy azurean waves crashed against the shore had a definite aesthetic appeal, the accompanying sound competed with her voice.

It doesn't matter.

The photographer could fill his roll of film with photos of her, and no magazine would buy them.

Not for her.

Not anymore.

The thought should have been the one joyful event of the day. Instead, her legs threatened to sway, but Cora gripped the railing in as nonchalant a manner as she could muster and glared at the man. "Go away. We don't like photographers."

For a brief second his eyes widened, and she smoothed her fringed leather dress. Perhaps she shouldn't have come straight from the studio. No doubt, her lasso and bright red Stetson also appeared ridiculous.

The stranger moved his camera away. "Very well, lassie."

Cora blinked.

Clearly, Veronica drew an international interest.

Not that that was unexpected.

The man winked at her, and she summoned her sternest look. "Go away."

He rose.

Leaves clung to the man's brown plaid suit. He dusted them off, and they floated slowly to the ground, as if unwilling to abandon him.

As far as men went, he was on the attractive end of the spectrum. Evidently, his time clambering in strangers' gardens had prevented him from suffering from muscle atrophy, and the exposure to California's good weather enabled one to term his skin sun-kissed.

Wrinkles marred his shirt collar, and his dark hair was too long. The fact should have made him less handsome. People commented dismissively about men who paid sporadic visits to their barber. And yet, the man could have rivaled any star in appearance. His attire compared unfavorably with the tailored finesse of the studio executives' suits.

He was a taller Clark Gable, a less polished Cary Grant.

Dark eyes twinkled at her, and she shoved her finger against the doorbell. When she glanced at him a second time, his lips had transformed into a smirk, as if he found her interest in entering the house unbelievable when she had the option of gazing at him.

Finally, the door swung open, and she hastened through the entry, stepping onto the black-and-white tiles. Potted citrus trees and their accompanying pleasant scent filled the foyer, and a large abstract painting hung in the hallway, denoting everything wonderful.

Cora should absolutely not be mulling the attractiveness of photographers.

They were a pest.

Always.

"There's a photographer outside," she blurted to Veronica's housekeeper. "In the garden."

She shouldn't feel guilty about the statement, but for some strange reason, she did anyway.

"*Ay, Dios mio.* I'll ring the guard."

"Good," Cora said, though her voice seemed caught at the top of her throat.

She turned around to see if the man might still be lingering on the other side of the glass door, but he was gone.

"Is that you, Cora?" Veronica's voice sounded from upstairs.

"Yes."

"Splendid!" Veronica strode down the staircase, and her platinum hair bounced. The abundant assortment of chandeliers imbued her in golden light as she descended the marble steps, and her silky ivory robe shimmered. Ostrich feathers lined the sleeves, billowing luxuriously, even though Cora was certain Veronica did not require the plumes for purposes of maintaining warmth.

"Heavens, what's wrong?" Veronica asked. "You look terrible." She wrinkled her nose. "I'm not sure fringe suits you, and the angle of a pert hat, for instance, is far more flattering—"

"The clothes are from the picture." Cora shifted her legs over the marble floor. Her boots squeaked, the sound amplified by the excellent acoustics.

"I see. Is there something wrong?"

"Yes," Cora squeaked.

If only there was a way she could avoid saying the words.

But not saying them wouldn't make them any less real.

Unfortunately.

"Darling, it's fine," Veronica said.

"Oh?" Cora blinked up at her, and Veronica nodded gravely.

"Everyone has a bad hair day sometimes. You can borrow my curling iron."

"Th-that's not it."

Veronica eyed her skeptically. "You can't disguise it."

Cora sighed. Perhaps her hair *was* frizzy.

"It's rather worse than that," she said.

"Oh, dear. I so wish we could have gone shopping together. It's a shame I'm leaving tomorrow. But perhaps—"

Cora shook her head.

"It isn't hopeless, my dear," Veronica said, in her typical worldly manner, even though she was only five months older than Cora.

There'd been a time when the studio had forced them to spend time together, hoping that Cora's goody two shoes reputation would help the public forget Veronica's wild one. The public had never forgotten, but somehow Veronica and Cora had become friends.

Unfortunately, even Veronica couldn't fix this.

"It's hopeless," Cora said.

"Did the studio say something?" Veronica asked.

"Not about my clothes..."

"Gee!" Veronica plopped down on an emerald tufted bench and clutched hold of the elaborate roll arm. "You don't mean to tell me that—"

She understood.

Thank goodness.

"I saw the signs," Veronica admitted. "But I can't believe they actually..." She moved her hand to her throat, slid her fingers over a shimmering ruby necklace, and then inhaled. "I can't believe they didn't invite you to Mr. Bellomo's birthday party."

"What?"

"That's it, isn't it?" Veronica asked. "I know it's mortifying to be considered so irrelevant."

"It's not that."

"Oh." Veronica exhaled. "I'm so pleased. That would have been truly, utterly terrible. I can't imagine anything worse. At your age, given your history. You know, I was worried for you when I didn't see your name appear at all in *Starlet Magazine* this year, and that reference in the *Jabberist* really didn't count since it was mostly about me, but..."

"They fired me," Cora said.

Veronica blinked. "Fired? For not being mentioned in any one of the gossip rags? That's ridiculous."

"That's not why they did it."

"But the studio's doing well!" Veronica exclaimed. "Better than ever! It even looks like we're going to leave this horrid depression."

"It's—" Shame filled Cora. "I don't think I'm meant to be an actress."

"But of course you are!"

"They didn't think so," Cora said softly.

"That's rubbish! You're in the middle of filming."

"They already hired my replacement."

"Who was it?"

"Some unknown girl. Mr. Bellomo discovered her in a coffee shop."

"My poor dear." Veronica bit her lower lip. "Perhaps they were being economical."

"Yes." Cora tried to say the phrase confidently and not reflect on the scores of errand boys and legions of other actresses on set. Hollywood seemed to be all about spending money and seemed to have little to do with restraint.

"There must be some mistake," Veronica said.

"Mr. Bellomo confirmed it to me himself." Cora's voice definitely wobbled now. Things like this weren't supposed to happen. Not with seven-year contracts. Not with people who'd achieved fame. She'd starred in pictures. She'd been "The Gal Detective." She hadn't expected—this. "He said I'd been chosen as a child actress for my ability to follow directions. To be still and learn my lines. And now—now I can't compete with the girls who went to high school, who experienced life..."

Cora yanked her purse open and grabbed hold of her handkerchief.

"Oh, honey." Veronica waved her hand in such a languid gesture that Cora wondered whether she'd practiced it.

Sometimes Cora thought it a pity that Veronica was slightly too young to have been a silent screen queen.

Veronica fluttered her fingers over her brow, and rings sparkled. "The world is really too cruel. One might expect it in Houston, but Hollywood? How positively horrid. We'll just figure something else for you. Fortunately, there are other studios in town. We'll get you to an even better one. MGM or Paramount. And you're quite a darling dancer. Maybe RKO will take you. You can play Ginger Rogers' rival in her films with Fred Astaire."

"I don't remember her ever having a rival—"

"All the better." Veronica's eyes glimmered, and Cora began to feel more hopeful.

Veronica was right.

There were other studios.

"You do have talent," said Veronica. "No matter what Mr. Bellomo says. You mustn't forget about that."

Cora nodded.

"Isn't it most exciting though?" Veronica beamed. "It's so important to have life experiences. Unemployment seems to be something so many people these days are facing."

"It's a Great Depression."

"But would I know it?" Veronica waved at her marble floors, crystal chandeliers, and modern furniture. "I read about it in the newspapers. But you, you can really experience it. So very worldly."

"I don't know what to do," Cora said. "I have to pay rent, and—"

"You do have your parents, honey. You're no orphan. Surely they can put you up while you look for something."

"I would rather not."

Veronica nodded thoughtfully.

Cora had considered petitioning to break away from her parents after they'd spent most of her money on furs, an always questionable purchase in Southern California, and cars, which had some practicality, though the curvaceous front fenders and glittering wheels were less necessary.

"I have rooms galore," Veronica said. "You could stay here."

Cora perked up.

"But... I might have to sell the property. Edmund's parents are quite tiresome. Most dismissive of Hollywood and its supposed lack of morals." Veronica's lips turned into a perfect pout. "You'd think they were really farmers in Wyoming and not members of the English aristocracy."

"They didn't approve of the elopement?"

"Honey, they abhorred it. They should be kneeling down before me, thanking me for saving them so much money for the wedding. Though I suppose they could afford it." Veronica smiled. "You could always hide under one of these gigantic beds if the house is sold. Call yourself the Ghost of Bel Air. Just fling over a white sheet if you see anyone." She clapped her hands. "I'll be sure to tell the gossip columnists that the place is haunted, so no one suspects it's merely an-out-of-work actress!"

"I'd rather not."

"Well, I suppose sheets are even less becoming than Stetson hats." Veronica tapped scarlet fingernails against a marble side table. "Perhaps you can come with me."

"To England?"

"Why naturally! Where else? Edmund will be delighted that I'll have company on the crossing. And it will be nice to have someone decent to speak to. Edmund's relatives are all so dreadful. Most unamused about absolutely everything."

Europe was miles away, filled with people who criticized the American way of doing things and from which emanated all manner of dramatic headlines.

"Just because you've developed an appalling habit of being boring, does not mean you have to remain that way. If I'd never changed..." Veronica's face took on a faraway look, and Cora wondered whether she was thinking of the sordid childhood she'd been rumored to have before being discovered. Veronica shook her head. "Well, we'll just have to fix that."

"I couldn't do that."

"Oh, do say you'll come. It will be most picturesque. Edmund's parents have a manor house in England. Quite remote from reporters. There will be snow and Christmas carolers and all those other things. It's in a place called Yorkshire, darling."

"It sounds cold."

"That's why blankets were invented, honey. Besides, isn't your grandmother English? It will be like coming home."

"She's my great aunt," Cora said, "and I've never met her."

"Then you must meet her," Veronica exclaimed. "Where does she live? London? York?"

"I believe a place called Sussex?"

Veronica's frown was instantaneous. "That's the very bottom of England. Apparently, it's pleasant, but from the pictures I've seen, the grass is a far paler shade than that of Yorkshire. One wonders whether it can be termed green at all. And I suppose great aunts can scarcely be considered family."

Cora nodded, though her stomach tightened uncomfortably.

Perhaps Great Aunt Maggie could scarcely be considered family, but apart from her parents, she was the only relative Cora had.

"You should still come with me. You'll be utterly anonymous." Veronica flashed two rows of well-maintained white teeth.

Anonymous.

Cora tested the word out in her mind, but the negative connotation seemed to roar back.

"How grand," she said. "But I'm not sure—"

"It will be such fun," Veronica hastened to say. "No press at all. You can go about in some dusty old tweed like the locals. Not a single sparkle. And at night, you can stay at Chalcroft Park. All quite smashing. And not in the least like a normal park. None of the picnic basket carrying crowd. Just a great big old house. It's terribly out of fashion—all turrets and gables, and it has loads of land that the sheep trim themselves."

"Isn't Europe supposed to be dangerous?"

"Utter nonsense. I know some journalists are quite insistent on depicting Hitler in the most revolting tones, but honestly, they're *writers.* It's practically their job to exaggerate! And they're old, and we all know how old people like to drone on and on and on about how much better things were in the past. Besides, think how much worse things were in the last generation. All those brawny farmers drowning in mud on dreary battlefields in Belgium and France. What could probably be worse? And those chemical attacks. Utterly monstrous. I'll take Hitler any day. Edmund's father can explain it all to you. He's quite passionate on the subject. One really mustn't be upset at them for wanting to rebuild their army after it got demolished in the last war."

"I suppose not," Cora said.

"Look, you can take my maid's place. I'd rather she went after me anyway so she can bring more things. Besides, I don't think you understand how dull it can be to travel. All those deserts and forests are attractive in their manner, but they're far better suited to paintings that one can glance at for a moment rather than as endless scenery. And then my new husband's family—" She sighed. "Really, you'll be helping me."

"I've never traveled farther east than Nevada. I've never even been on a plane."

Veronica widened her eyes. "Well, that settles it. You're coming with me."

Chapter Two

DESPITE WHAT VERONICA said about flying being a common occurrence, flying felt anything but natural. The aircraft flitted by tangerine-tinged clouds. The propellers roared in Cora's ears, and the plane jostled as it pushed through more clouds.

She was going to England.

It was really happening.

Modern buildings stretched majestically toward the sky, and slate blue waters glittered below.

Veronica leaned over Cora. "That's our ship!"

It was the largest one in the water, though it looked worryingly small beside the skyscrapers.

The plane rattled, and Cora tightened her grip on her armrests.

Veronica downed the vodka drink the stewardess had given her and pulled out a silver cigarette case. Her crimson fingernails flashed as she inserted a cigarette into a jade holder and lit up. The ashy smoke wasn't able to hamper the view as the plane descended from the clouds. Pursing her ruby red painted lips around the holder, she inhaled deeply, and gray ash toppled onto Cora's lap.

Before, Cora could react, Veronica brushed it away. "Sorry." Her voice seemed tighter, more constrained than normal, and Cora jerked her head toward her friend. Perhaps Veronica was nervous about flying after all.

The plane glided to the ground and came to a halt, and Cora followed Veronica down the metal steps. Cora got a fleeting glimpse of a two-story brick building with a windowed tower set in the front center, before they were ushered into a taxi that sped them toward lower Manhattan.

The clouds shifted, and the sun splashed bright light over the buildings. Glass windows sparkled Steam rose from the gutters, but the burst of fog seemed to only imbue the atmosphere with added intensity.

This did not resemble California.

The palm trees were missing.

They'd been replaced with trees that had thicker trunks and possessed a multitude of branches, but none of them managed to retain many leaves. Any that remained were orange or brown, wrinkled or dead. The palm trees in California faced no such difficulty, and Cora felt a pang for their slender forms and the graceful arch of their leaves.

Cora shifted in her seat, unnerved by the height of the buildings. They couldn't possibly stand hundreds of stories effortlessly.

Tall buildings existed in both Vegas and Los Angeles, but not at this height, and the open expanse of land in those places had never made the buildings seem claustrophobic. These buildings were huddled together as though seeking strength from each other.

The taxi wove quickly through the streets, lurching from corner to corner, as if each opening of space between the cars and carriages was a lifeline.

"It's so different," Cora exclaimed.

Veronica smirked. "Wait until we reach England."

Cora nodded, but a prickle of nervousness coursed through her.

Perhaps her great aunt lived in England, but Cora had never met her, and she certainly didn't know anything about the country except that the colonials had found the English sufficiently unappealing that they'd waged a revolution to free themselves.

It seemed foolish for an American to venture there.

Californians weren't even supposed to feel at home on the East Coast.

As the taxi continued its rush through the city traffic, street children stepped out of the way. Dirt stained their clothes and tangled hair.

"How horrible," Cora said.

"They'll be fine." Veronica averted her gaze abruptly. "It will be awfully grand to be on the ship. So much velvet, dear. And the crimson kind."

"Just like the theater."

"Yes," Veronica purred. "Oh, you do understand. Though I've never been quite partial to red velvet attire. Blues and greens are so much more mysterious. And one must be mysterious."

Veronica continued to chatter merrily over the merits of various hues and tints, not returning her gaze to the window until they reached Central Park, and the urchins had been replaced with strolling ladies in fur coats and embroidered hats.

Cora frowned. She knew so little about Veronica's childhood.

The mothers of the other child stars had practically resided on set, but not Veronica's.

She turned her gaze to the window.

Men marched on the streets in long woolen coats. Shoes with spats peeked from their business suits. Beside them women strode purposefully, swathed in fur-collared tweed and swinging glossy alligator handbags.

These men and women were not going to work before the bright lights or in the dimmer environs of the backstage. It seemed strange to see a city so large not reliant on the entertainment industries.

For a moment, jealousy coursed through Cora. What would it be like to be one of those women? Or even to work for one of them?

The idea seemed almost appealing. She wouldn't worry then about photographers following her, and she wouldn't need to recite romantic lines to an actor she'd just met before a large crew.

But then Cora remembered the crash. Wall Street and New York City had played a role in ushering in the Great Depression. It was better to be wary of the place, with the narrow gaps between its buildings, and the seeming never-ending bustle of people.

The taxi turned toward the river. Boats and ships dotted the almost gray water. Cora missed California's turquoise waves, studded with foamy white spray.

The taxi finally stopped. "We're here," announced the driver.

Cora waited for him to open the door and then stepped out.

The RMS Queen Mary seemed calm, a beacon of elegance and sumptuousness against the tightly crammed buildings. The scarlet smokestacks adorned it with the magnificence of a crown, and people thronged upon the decks.

"Why, it's Veronica James!" someone shouted, and a crowd of journalists rushed toward them.

"How does it feel to be a countess?" one journalist asked.

"Glorious." Veronica twirled around, and Cora wondered if her sharply angled felt hat might fly off.

"Such a fairy tale," another person exclaimed.

In her element, Veronica beamed.

It was a fairy tale.

Earls normally married English debutantes, when they bothered to marry at all. They weren't supposed to marry Americans.

"How did you like your last time in Hollywood?" a third journalist shouted.

Veronica's smile wobbled. "I'll miss you, America."

The others laughed. "Nah. No way."

"I still have one more film to make," she said quickly. "After Christmas."

"You won't come back," a reporter called to her. "Not when you're reunited with your earl."

"Who wants an autograph?" Veronica asked, and an excited murmur rippled through the crowd.

Cora frowned.

How happy was Veronica that she was giving up her career for marriage?

Likely, she was reading too much into it.

Unlike Cora, Veronica had chosen to leave. The decision was obvious to anyone. Why be an actress when one could be a countess?

They ascended the gangway, and Veronica murmured that they were lucky that they would be sailing so late in the year and the ship was not full. Most people didn't want to submit themselves to the whims of the ocean, and Veronica had been able to procure one of the nicer cabins.

They strode over lush red carpets that covered the floors, as if the ship were attempting to mimic a grand hotel and was not the main method of transportation to the continent. Hopefully the long pile of the carpets had not been selected as necessary padding for a tumultuous crossing.

"Tell me more about the hosts," Cora said. "I've never met a duke and duchess."

"But you are on very intimate terms with a countess." Veronica winked.

Cora smiled. She imagined the duke and duchess's lives involved a great deal of jewels and permanently upturned noses.

Veronica released a sigh. "They are perhaps not the most pleasant of hosts."

"Oh?"

"Well, hospitality is hardly an English trait. They see their role as more of reminding people of their importance. To think, one day Edmund will be a duke, and I will be his duchess."

The magazines were already celebrating that fact.

"Do tell me more about Chalcroft Park," Cora said.

Veronica shrugged. "It's *called* a park darling, but I must admit, it looks more like a castle. Though technically it's a manor house."

"Smashing." Cora tried to lean back casually and replicate some of Veronica's nonchalance.

"It's beautiful." Veronica's eyes sparkled, and her lips spread into a wide smile.

It was perhaps difficult, even for a Hollywood movie star, to act entirely nonchalant about the prospect of turrets and moats.

"Who will be there?" Cora asked

"You'll meet Edmund of course." Veronica gave Cora a blissful smile that seemed incongruent with the man's pompous name.

Cora had seen pictures of him in newspapers and magazines, and she was happy to be able to meet him in person. All the articles had lauded him, praising his attractiveness. His receding hairline and weak chin seemed unlikely attributes in a cover model, but Cora supposed aristocrats had different standards to meet. Simply being under forty seemed a cause for celebration.

"What are his parents like?" Cora asked. "Does he have siblings?"

"An older half-brother. His father was a bit of a scoundrel in his past, and Rhys won't be inheriting anything. And Edmund's parents are—" Veronica paused, and for the second time Cora wondered if she was truly happy moving to England.

It had seemed odd that she'd been so eager to bustle her off and join her for Christmas.

"I mean...they're fine," Veronica said. "Naturally."

Cora waited for her to continue.

"His father is quite old. I imagine he will likely pass away soon."

"How unfortunate."

Veronica blinked. "Oh, yes. Of course."

"Though sometimes appearances can be deceiving," Cora said, trying to be reassuring. "Perhaps he'll reach a hundred. I imagine dukes have quite wonderful doctors."

"Er—yes." Veronica rang the bell for an attendant and seemed relieved when he arrived. "Can you please make sure my maid is settled properly? And bring us drinks."

"Something refreshing?"

"Something strong." She gave the attendant a tip and turned back to Cora. "It won't be just the family. Audrey will be there of course. Lady Audrey, I should say. They do so insist on using their titles." Veronica gave a slight grimace, a gesture Cora thought she'd reserved purely for the most appalling news headlines. Veronica was careful to minimize the formation of future wrinkles.

"Who is Lady Audrey?" Cora asked.

"I believe the term they use in England is 'bright young thing.' Perfectly ghastly, if you ask me. As if the rest of us are not nearly as bright. She'll be painting my portrait—she's already working on one for the duchess."

Cora doubted that Audrey's supposed intelligence was what was causing Veronica grief. Veronica used to tease the more studious of girls on the lot, and certainly seemed disinclined to emulate, much less be mistaken for them.

"How did you meet her?"

"Edmund knows her. She lived in a nearby manor house, and I gather they climbed apple trees together and watched frogs jump or some such idyllic nonsense. Now she lives in London, but she expressed nostalgia, and poor Edmund is such a sweet man—really, such a sweet, sweet man, that he invited her. To our first Christmas together." She put her arms on her hips and glared, as if she were auditioning for the role of head fury in some Grecian tragedy.

"I'm sorry."

Veronica shrugged. "What you must think of me, honey. And she's not so bad. In fact—you must spend time with her. Heaps of time."

Cora nodded. She had the vague impression she'd been invited there to rectify a third wheel by becoming a fourth one. She could do fourth wheels though. It was two wheels that she had more trouble with. Her dates had been limited to publicity stunts, where she'd been chosen more for her reliability and disinclination to sell salacious gossip than for any compatibility.

"Who else is coming?" Cora asked.

"Rhys Ardingley and his wife Katherine. She's in a wheelchair and terribly prone to petulance. It doesn't help that they're both impoverished. Rhys has never gotten over the fact that he's the duke's eldest son but isn't actually allowed to inherit anything." She shrugged. "At least the duke acknowledges him. And apparently, some Italian man is coming too, Edmund says. He has some sort of business dealings with the duke."

"I see."

"You'll adore England," Veronica said. "Not the people, naturally. Far too conceited."

Cora hid her smile. Veronica seemed an unlikely person to be outraged by a well-developed superiority complex.

"The countryside there is decent," Veronica mused, and Cora followed her gaze to the tiny porthole. Cora glanced around. She had to admit, despite the well-appointed comfort of the stateroom, it was a bit cramped for space.

Veronica jumped up. "Let's explore the rest of the ship."

Cora followed her out. People crowded around them as they entered the first-class lounge. Businessmen surged around them, and Cora was once again conscious that she was traveling far away from her home.

"Aren't you scared of overeager men?" Cora whispered.

"Oh, you are really rather too uptight," she said. "It was fine when you were younger, but you're becoming set in your ways. What you need is a nice man. Someone like Edmund."

"I doubt I will find one with your new relatives."

She laughed. "Edmund's older half-brother is extremely dashing." Her smile faded into a thoughtful pout. "Though quite married. Perhaps Edmund has a friend. Perhaps someone he plays squash with on a regular basis. Or perhaps...polo." She gazed up at the sky, and her eyes glimmered, in a way that only experienced women were accustomed to doing.

Cora did not belong to that category.

"As for protection, the best defense is a good offense." Veronica raised her skirt in a seductive manner, and wolf whistles sounded.

"Veronica," Cora hissed, but Veronica only lifted the hem higher.

Cora rolled her eyes. A holster was strapped to Veronica's thigh, and from it, she removed a mother-of-pearl hilted dagger.

Cora's mouth dropped open.

Veronica laughed. "Honey, it's important to take care of oneself. Much less complicated than a pistol, but equally effective. Just be sure to select a single-edged knife. You wouldn't want to hurt yourself. I must be sure you get one."

"That's not necessary," Cora said quickly. "Put that back. And let's find some seats."

They wove through the crowd of sumptuously attired people. Veronica seemed to be enjoying the enthusiastic whispers that happened when they approached the bar and finally stopped lauding the wonders of weaponry. The ship whisked them away to everything wonderful, and Cora tried to not concentrate on the fact that she also was leaving America and everything she knew.

THE SHIP HAD TOSSED and turned with predictable unpleasantness for the whole of the voyage, and they were now nearing Southampton.

Veronica had seemed happy to confine herself to the cabin, and even her always generous application of makeup hadn't quite masked the unfashionable green pallor that could only have been generated from thousands of waves pressing against the ship in a multitude of fashions, all distasteful.

On occasion, Cora would hear Veronica's gramophone stream in from the other side of the wooden walls. She was practicing for her last film, an adaption of a radio play that had become popular.

The film would be her last; countesses weren't known for a propensity for performing in Hollywood, and Veronica would be no exception.

Cora sighed. Perhaps one of the other studios would offer her a contract. Likely it wouldn't be very impressive, not once news of her firing from Mr. Bellomo's studio made the rounds, but any contract was better than no contract.

She just needed the gossip to clear.

Once the other directors no longer read negative stories, then surely everything would be fine.

It has to be.

Cora pushed away the thought that perhaps acting wasn't something she actually wanted to do.

Some musings were irrelevant.

She wasn't suited to anything else except acting. She might have had a tutor on set, but she would hardly be seen as well-educated by others. Most people hadn't been taught algebra in five-minute increments.

Finally, the ship's horn sounded.

"We're here," Veronica said gaily.

Cora followed Veronica down the gangplank, this time to a whole new country, a whole new world.

"Unmoving ground," Veronica declared. "My favorite thing."

"It does seem an excellent quality," Cora agreed, uncertain about what other qualities this place had.

"I'll wire Edmund once we get the train schedule to let him know we're arriving early. He'll be so happy," Veronica said.

The train ride to York was a blur, involving a night in London. Cora was vaguely aware of conductors in brightly colored uniforms and people clutching timetables. Clearly, they weren't the only people traveling far for the Christmas holidays.

The train rushed over the countryside, unhampered now by having to stop in many towns; in fact, there didn't seem to be any.

No snow was present, though some people spoke of an upcoming storm.

The trees were bare, and the sky gray. Brown leaves covered the ground, and the grass was a similar dull color. On occasion, tall trees arched gnarly branches toward the cloud-spattered heavens. They sat majestically, incognizant they hadn't been replaced with a vegetable patch merely because of their location on the property's border.

Stone manor homes seemed to crown each hill, overseeing the inconsistently sized fields and small cottages covered with soot.

"From the coal mines," Veronica explained, apparently noticing Cora's gaze. "It's on everything. Edmund's family owns a mine. It's the largest in England."

"How impressive."

Veronica's cheeks pinkened, and she dipped her head downward and fumbled in her bag.

"You seem so proud," Cora teased.

"Nonsense." Veronica removed her powder case and began retouching makeup that already looked immaculate. She glanced back at Cora. "You were supposed to stop smiling. It's just, I might be famous—"

"Very famous."

"But Edmund—he's respectable. He comes from a good family. Perhaps it's silly, but I quite like being associated with it. Imagine, we're having Christmas in the same manor house that his family has been having Christmas in for generations."

"And he's an earl," Cora added.

"And one day, he'll be a duke," Veronica said, her voice once again decidedly dreamy.

The train slowed.

"We're here." Veronica stood, and Cora followed her to the train's exit.

The station was empty.

"I imagine Edmund is waiting in the car," Veronica said. "The man despises crowds. How do I look?"

"Perfect."

She beamed. "It is perhaps silly to ask, but this is a big moment. It's been two months since I last saw him."

Veronica practically skipped from the platform, and Cora picked up both of their bags. The air felt heavy and frigid, and she was glad when her traveling companion stopped beneath an awning to survey the station.

She followed Veronica under a Victorian awning. Swirls and floral shapes had been formed into the metal, and she glanced upward.

"If you think that's impressive, honey," Veronica drawled, "wait until you see the house."

"Perhaps I should get the smelling salts out," Cora said.

"Perhaps."

A short man in a uniform and funny hat stepped onto the platform and swept into a deep bow. "Ah, Lady Holt." He turned to Cora. "And Miss Clarke, is it?"

Cora nodded, as the man once again moved his torso toward the ground.

"What's your name?"

The man laughed. "I am what they call the local constable. I make this area safe. Constable Kirby, at your service."

Cora glanced around, taking in the sharply sloped hills. Stone walls, which looked like they had been constructed centuries before, were the only buildings.

She'd never been to a more isolated area.

"Surely it cannot be very dangerous here?"

"Don't you worry." The constable ran his fingers over the lapels of his coat, and his lips spread into a wide smile. "No murderer dares make trouble here. Now, Lady Holt, would you like me to drive you two to Chalcroft Park?

"How very kind of you," Veronica murmured. "But I am certain that my husband is here."

"Right. Naturally." The man's eyes glazed, as most men seemed to do in Veronica's presence, as if they were in the midst of admiring the planes of her face and the wide placement of her large blue eyes, rather than devoting energy to listening to her.

"Would you like an autograph?" Veronica said benevolently.

Her question did not seem to have the desired effect.

The pace at which the constable's face became red seemed too brisk. "It's—er—possible I may not have actually seen you in the movies."

"No?"

"Though I would have if I'd known you would become the new countess," the man rushed to add. "The family is most important. Some people don't like them, because of all the deaths they caused in the last century, but I think it's splendid that we've got our own duke and duchess now. Makes this region seem right proper. Just like York. Even Harrogate doesn't have its own duke."

"Oh," Veronica's smile wobbled. "That's nice."

Cora frowned. "What deaths did the family cause?"

The constable opened his mouth, but Veronica pulled her forward. "I think that's my husband! Let's go."

A red candy-colored Rolls Royce sat outside the train station.

"Is that the car?"

"It must be new," Veronica said. "Look how exquisite it is."

The cream-colored wheels and silver grating contrasted beautifully with the car's vibrant color.

"Edmund!" Veronica called out.

A head peeked from the window.

A head that seemed distinctly...unmasculine.

Veronica halted, and her face whitened. "Audrey. I mean—Lady Audrey."

The woman waved. "Yes, my dear."

Veronica smiled, but no matter how many acting accolades she'd received, the smile was too tight. A director would have scolded her for it, but this was real life, and Veronica continued toward Lady Audrey.

The woman was perhaps in her early thirties. Her hair was cut in an unfashionable, practical bob, as if she were still in the last decade and was not aware that everyone was growing out their hair into softer waves. Cora wondered if the short length was more to prohibit needing to style her hair than for a desire to be dramatic. Lady Audrey's skin was tanned and freckled, and she wore a checked tweed jacket that looked like it had seen several seasons. Cora felt overdressed in her fur-collared coat, though she couldn't afford the triple strand of pearls that dangled casually around Lady Audrey's neck. Some paint was splattered on her gloves, and Cora remembered that she was an artist.

The woman rose languidly and waved an elegant hand vaguely in their direction. "It is a pleasure to see you again, Lady Holt."

"How nice to see you, Lady Audrey," Veronica said.

Veronica might be a great actress, and she may even have been nominated for an Oscar once, but she wasn't even attempting to curve her lips into a smile. They were pressed together in icy formality.

Lady Audrey moved her fingers through her hair, as if to smooth it, but she only managed to make her bob appear more misshapen. Cora couldn't help but feel sorry for her.

"I do hope you have a good time, Miss Clarke," Lady Audrey said, directing her attention away from Veronica. "Do ignore our stodgy habits."

"I'm sure you don't have any."

"Nonsense. I certainly couldn't imagine being in Hollywood."

"It does require an abundance of glamor," Veronica mused, and Lady Audrey's face blushed pink, despite her ample freckles.

"You must show me your painting sometime," Cora said, changing the subject.

Most artists Cora knew were happy to show people their work, extrapolating over the wonders of their composition technique or color palette.

"Perhaps you can show us once we arrive?" Veronica said sweetly. "Goodness knows we can use some culture after our long period of travel."

"Um—" If Lady Audrey normally displayed poise, she seemed to have a dearth of it now.

"Where is my husband?" Veronica asked.

"Edmund's at Chalcroft Park. He would have loved to have fetched you, but the man is busy."

"Naturally," Veronica said tersely.

The car sped over narrow roads. At times steep hedges loomed on either side, obscuring the landscape, as if to ensure Lady Audrey would not decide to suddenly pull the vehicle into a vegetable patch.

The trees fared no better than those in New York. The few present seemed to consist entirely of dark brown trunks and branches. Their leaves, when they had any, were shriveled up and a dull orange, as if somebody had set fire to them, instead of them simply being battered by the obviously incessant blustery wind. A few pine trees stood in the distance, but their green needles, which pointed downward, hardly sufficed in bringing more color to the world.

"It's good you came before the snow," Lady Audrey said.

Cora glanced at the sky, trying to discern any snowflakes, but all she saw were thick clouds in varying degrees of gray.

Shortly after, though, snow began drifting down, smattering over every slope.

The car swept through valleys, avoiding the occasional steep hill, until finally it clambered upward.

Veronica pointed. "Chalcroft Park."

Cora followed the direction of Veronica's finger. The hill seemed empty, but a sliver of pale gray grew steadily larger.

Gray should have been a dull color, but the manor house looked more imposing than anything she'd ever seen.

"It's beautiful," Cora breathed, taking in turrets and gables. It even had a moat.

The landscape here seemed more solemn, almost primeval.

Majestic trees jutted from the groomed lawn. Gold leaves shimmered under the setting sun, crowning the almost bare lofty branches in glory as snow fluttered down elegantly.

The wheels crunched on gravel, and Lady Audrey stopped the engine. They exited the car as servants rushed toward them.

Chapter Three

The manor house was even more splendid on close perusal, and Cora felt every bit as naïve as the people who arrived in Hollywood from rural communities in geometrically shaped states. Everything appeared fascinating, even though Cora had the distinct impression most visitors here might not wonder at the beauty of the pond or the long stretches of grass, broken up only by majestic chestnut trees.

Cora tilted her head upward, enjoying the whispering of the wind. Tips of the slopes seemed to recede into the dark gray sky.

"They say Yorkshire is God's country," Lady Audrey said, perhaps observing Cora's delight. "It's the closest thing to perfect."

"That must explain why you're here, and not in London with the rest of your set," Veronica said.

Lady Audrey's face fell, and Cora sighed.

Veronica could be brusque. She tended to view most women with suspicion.

Perhaps Veronica didn't like Lady Audrey, but Cora had known Veronica long enough to know that that did not necessarily have anything to do with Lady Audrey's personality.

"It was kind of you to pick us up," Cora assured Lady Audrey.

"I thought you might prefer me to a servant. They are grumbling about snow so much, though these snowflakes scarcely seem threatening."

"I've never seen snow before," Cora confessed.

"You really are American," Lady Audrey said. "How charming! So very quaint."

"I mean, I've seen it on the tops of mountains on occasion," Cora said. "But I've never touched it."

"You can do so now," Lady Audrey said.

"Yes," Cora said. "It's wet and cold and—"

"Just like snow," Veronica said drily. "I'm going to find Edmund."

She headed toward the entrance, and they followed her over a small bridge that extended over a moat.

"It's a castle," Cora exclaimed.

"It is not old enough to have been used for defensive purposes. And some wings of the home are positively respectable. No turrets at all."

The butler opened the door before they reached it. The house might seem grandiose, and it certainly was, but Cora shivered, conscious of the possible appearance of people from behind the dark wooden columns.

"Lady Holt," the butler said. He held the door, shoulders square and chin stoic. His ebony uniform seemed to soak up the ambient light shining from the hallway. With his dark clothing and dour expression, he appeared as though he was perpetually prepared for anything, even sudden tragedies.

"Welcome."

"Hello, Wexley. This is my friend, Cora Clarke."

"Welcome to Chalcroft Park." The butler lowered his torso into a bow and managing to imbue his baritone voice with gravitas. "I hope you find your stay amenable."

Cora followed Veronica inside.

The place retained its fairytale look inside.

Stained glass windows cast blue and red reflections of prettily patterned flowers and plants onto dark wooden floorboards that gleamed from obviously carefully applied polish. Majestic Victorian furniture dotted the hall, and Cora felt like she'd stepped onto a set of the very most expensive production, but unlike those, this was absolutely real.

"It's like a dream," she murmured.

"I feel the same way," Veronica whispered.

Veronica's worldliness made it easy to forget that she'd come from an impoverished background, but in moments like this, Cora remembered it.

And now she was wed to an earl, she was a countess, and one day she would become a duchess.

This whole place would be hers.

It was so heavenly. So exquisite. So perfect.

Cora tried to absorb every single detail.

This wasn't just a set that would be dismantled a week later. This wasn't just a prettily painted backdrop, and the people were not just wearing the same clothes that they'd worn on a different movie.

No.

This was real life.

And it was perfect.

"Are you trailing snow into the house?" a voice boomed.

Cora stiffened, and Veronica swirled around.

An elderly man in a burgundy robe tottered on the landing above them. He had a thick mustache and the cord of his monocle flapped against his gaunt face. He grasped hold of the bannister, as if he'd managed to assign most of his energy to scowling rather than standing.

Veronica raised her chin. "It's hardly snowed at all."

"You should not do that," he continued. "The floors are old."

"A little water won't hurt them," Veronica said in her normal breezy voice. "It's nothing they don't go through when they're being cleaned."

The man's already wrinkled nose developed new creases, and he huffed. "This house wouldn't have survived if my ancestors had possessed such a flippant, *American* attitude."

Veronica inhaled, and if Cora did not know that Veronica despised arithmetic, she would have thought she was counting.

"Your grace," Veronica said, "may I please present my dearest friend, Miss Cora Clarke?"

This is the duke?

No wonder Veronica had termed him to be not very welcoming.

Cora sank into an awkward curtsy.

"Hmph," the duke muttered and wandered away. His slippers squeaked on the landing above.

A maid appeared to assist Veronica and Cora in removing the offending coats and boots that had caused the duke such distress.

The door opened behind them, and Lady Audrey appeared.

"Where were you?" Veronica asked.

"Just parking the car," Lady Audrey said.

"Right." Veronica frowned. "Let's go."

Cora followed Veronica into the drawing room.

The room smelled deliciously of pine needles. Garlands were strung about the ceiling, and a large Christmas tree shimmered with brightly colored ornaments.

"Darling!" a man's voice sounded, and Veronica's whole face lit up.

She dashed toward the newcomer, and he spun her around in his sturdy arms.

"I've missed you," he said.

"This is Cora Clarke," Veronica said, still resting in his embrace. "She was one of the actresses with whom I worked for years."

"Pleased to meet you," murmured Cora.

"How was your journey?" he asked.

"The ship was far too slow." Veronica tilted her head up to him as if for him to kiss her, but he gave her a peck on her cheek.

"The servants are around," Lord Holt said.

"Oh." Veronica managed to look confused, but her husband squeezed her hands.

"You can greet my mother." He led them to the other side of the room.

For some reason, Cora had expected Veronica's husband to be more dynamic. Lord Holt was tall, but his amble seemed hesitant, as if his limbs resented their extra length. Veronica had a habit of being linked to the most smashing male leads, the men who graced magazines with maddening frequency, even though they never seemed to manage to have so much as a shirt to accompany them on their photo shoots.

No doubt Lord Holt's title and wealth made up for his lack of regular features and the absence of a chin, and perhaps he thought the utter absence of imperfections on Veronica's features might render handsome children.

Lord Holt halted before a woman. "Mother, may I present Miss Cora Clarke? Miss Clarke this is Her Grace, the Duchess of Hawley"

"How do you do?" the woman said, scarcely lifting her gaze from her book, and Cora noted the trace of an Eastern European accent.

Cora had been expecting a woman with gray hair to match that of the duke, but the duchess had rich auburn hair. She had none of her son's uncertainty and wore a bold emerald dress that highlighted slender ankles. The dress was likely Parisian, instead of the kind hastily made from cheap, if shiny, fabric favored by budget-conscious Hollywood producers.

Veronica tossed her hair. "Hello, Ma."

The woman's exquisitely plucked eyebrows rose and for a moment, Cora thought the duchess would roll her eyes. Instead, the duchess gave Veronica an icy smile. "I do hope you enjoyed the elopement."

"A night with your son—what's not to adore?" Veronica asked.

The duchess swallowed hard.

Voices sounded from the foyer.

"Ah... It must be the Italian gentleman." The duchess rushed toward the door, hurrying over the Oriental carpets. "Signor Palombi! Welcome."

A man stepped into the room. Cora had envisioned him with a forceful attitude and a bulging figure that came from making business deals over steak.

The man she saw did not seem to possess either of those qualities. His figure was trim, and his facial features were of such regular size that they could, like the Duchess of Hawley's bone structure, be termed pleasing.

Cora's lips twitched.

The man was the most stereotypical sort of Italian. Her own father was Italian American and was a singer in Las Vegas. The studio had decided that her mother's name was more appropriate for an actress. His career had grown with Cora's, and he had needed larger and larger rooms to fill with starry-eyed fans as he belted Italian songs few could even understand.

Signor Palombi swept his gaze across the room, and Cora had the impression that not a single candlestick or teacup would go unnoticed.

"Why this is *magnifico*," he declared.

"I'm so glad you like it." The duchess beamed and clasped her hands to her heart.

Lord Holt stiffened. Perhaps he thought his mother was behaving in an almost besotted fashion.

"Archibald will like it too," Signor Palombi said.

"He brought another guest?" A scowl formed on Lord Holt's face.

"Archibald! Stop inspecting the foyer," Signor Palombi exclaimed, and pitter-patters sounded.

An adorable small dog with curly white fur stepped into the room.

"He's lovely," the duchess said, bending down to greet the four-legged guest.

Edmund stiffened. "I'll make sure the rooms are prepared."

"I'll come with you," Veronica said quickly.

They left the drawing room, and after a few minutes of conversation with the duchess, the Italian gentleman joined Cora.

"My name is Achille Palombi." He swept himself into a bow. "You are lovely. A friend of the famous actress?"

"We acted as children together."

"Are you performing anything now?"

"Not for the time being," Cora admitted.

"Then enjoy Christmas," the Italian said. "I am told that the English do an excellent Christmas pudding."

The dog tilted his head at Cora, as if assessing her, and then strode up to her and licked her shoes.

"Forgive Archibald," Signor Palombi said. "He has evidently determined that your shoes have traveled far. He's never been to California."

"His name is Archibald?" she asked.

"Ah yes," Signor Palombi said. "I've always desired to have an English name myself."

"I didn't know Italians were fond of the English," she said. "What with Mussolini and all."

Signor Palombi's smile wobbled. "I like the gravitas in his name."

"Archibald does sound rather venerable," Cora agreed.

The dog twirled around, perhaps delighted at being described as respectable.

"I see I was not the last to arrive," Signor Palombi said.

Cora followed the Italian's gaze to the doorway.

A man with gray speckled hair and a mustache entered the drawing room. His features seemed composed entirely of chiseled planes: a sturdy jaw, high cheekbones and a nose that managed to not slope up or down. Mr. Bellomo would have dragged him to the casting couch. The strands of silver did not hide the man's handsomeness.

"Miss Clarke, isn't it?" the man said. "You must be the other starlet."

"Indeed."

"A pleasure." His voice was also polished. How did the British manage to make the simplest words sound heavenly? Her mind drifted once again to the strange photographer.

"My name is Rhys Ardingley," the newcomer said.

"I'm glad someone fun is here," Veronica called from the landing. Veronica hurried down the steps, and Lord Holt followed her at a more sedate pace. "We're going to have a riot. Cora, meet my brother-in-law."

"The black sheep, I'm afraid," he said. "Older, but Father was naughty and didn't marry my mother."

"Don't scare her," Veronica warned. "This is her first time out of the country."

"An ingénue!" Mr. Ardingley tapped his hand over his heart, and his eyes widened. "And you've chosen my father's house to make your foreign debut?"

"Likely an honor he does not appreciate," a female voice said.

Mr. Ardingley's smile tightened. "Katherine. I did not see you."

"Oh, just look down and behind you. That's generally where I am."

"Right." Mr. Ardingley's voice croaked, and he stepped away.

A woman with dark curly hair and thick eyebrows worthy of Joan Crawford sat in a wheelchair.

"Miss Clarke, please let me present my darling wife," Mr. Ardingley said smoothly.

"Oh, you needn't act so romantic," Mrs. Ardingley said, pushing down on the wheels to propel herself forward. "Any fool can tell you're not devoted, and we're in the presence of two actresses. They can see past your lines. They probably don't even consider them well-delivered. I certainly don't."

Mr. Ardingley's earlier cocky grin vanished.

The woman thrust her hand out to Cora. "Welcome to Chalcroft Park. I see you're the uninvited guest."

"I invited her," Veronica said quickly. "Cora is my dearest, most darling friend."

"Hmph." Mrs. Ardingley continued to scrutinize her.

"Perhaps we should retire," Veronica said hastily. "We had a long voyage."

"Dinner is at eight," Lord Holt said.

"I remember."

"Good." He nodded curtly and turned away.

When she looked at Veronica, her cheeks had grown somewhat pink. "Edmund is the strong and silent type."

Cora nodded. Perhaps the man made up for any lack of strength with an excess of silence.

"And he is an earl," Veronica said again, sliding her hand around Cora's arm. "Let's go upstairs."

They ascended the steps and entered a long hall. The chairs were pressed against the sides of one wall. The heavy carved furniture seemed discordant with the cozy environment she expected of a home. Still, this was going to be a wonderful visit.

Chapter Four

The formality in the house extended into Cora's bedroom. The room might lack the animal print upholstery and gold and silver detailing favored by Hollywood's elite, but the domed canopy bed and the floral curtains draped upon it must be expensive. Matching curtains lined the windows, though these were topped with stiff pelmets. The busy pattern seemed at odds with the increasingly white landscape outside.

Cora strode to the window.

Golly.

The snow was positively racing downward, as if each flake had decided to enter the Grand Prix. Cold air hurtled through cracks in the aged windowpane, and she glanced longingly at the large stone fireplace that dominated one wall. A thick Oriental screen was placed in front of it, presumably to protect from any wayward sparks. Not that any sparks were happening now; the room was chilly. She moved toward the bed, eyeing the abundant compilation of coverlets, bedspreads, quilts, and duvets with pleasure.

Perhaps she might rest.

Just for a bit.

Cora removed her shoes, sat down on the bed, and soon found her eyelids seeming to grow heavy. She lay down and pulled the covers about her.

And perhaps, just perhaps, she slept.

A knock sounded, and Cora jerked her torso up.

The door swung open.

Cora pushed away the covers. "Veronica?"

"It's only me, ma'am," a stern voice said. "The maid. One of them."

Cora scrambled up, and the blanket lay crumpled around her legs.

A middle-aged woman scrutinized her. She wore a bulky black dress, the color evidently not muted from frequent washings, and a crisp white apron. A lace cap perched on her head. "You should have rung for me." She pointed to the silk rope that hung from the ceiling.

"I—"

"I'll make a fire for you," the maid said. "Even if these aren't conventional hours."

"That's really not necessary," Cora declared.

"Can't have you sleeping under the covers with your afternoon dress on."

Cora wouldn't have referred to a dark blue frock as an afternoon dress, but clearly this was the sort of place where one changed for dinner, even if one were merely going downstairs, and not to some riveting new club or movie opening.

Another maid entered the room.

Her uniform was every bit as meticulous, though she was younger than the other maid and wore rouge and lipstick. She stared at Cora.

Cora knew that look.

"I can dress her," the new maid said.

"I never thought you were eager to add more duties," the first maid said.

"I am now."

"Very well."

Cora was somewhat glad when the first maid left the room. She'd seemed rather too reminiscent of the school teacher who had taught Cora on the sets of movies, pulling her into a classroom with Veronica and some other child actors, whenever the adults were on break.

They'd studied arithmetic and reading, while the adults laughed and sipped cocktails.

Cora had had no desire to sip cocktails in those days, but she'd still been scared of the schoolteacher who'd seemed to work from the assumption that child actors were spoiled, even though unlike most other children, they all worked hard.

"I'm Gladys," the new maid said.

"And I'm—"

"Cora Clarke." Gladys's eyes shimmered. "It's such a pleasure to meet you, miss. Now let's get you dressed."

Cora rose from the bed, still groggy from the hours of travel.

"I've seen every one of your films, miss."

"I hope you enjoyed them."

"Oh, naturally. Seeing you tap dance on the ceiling. Really, too brilliant."

Cora smiled.

Gladys glanced at Cora's feet, perhaps half expecting her to burst into dance.

"Let me unpack for you," Gladys said. "You must have all sorts of lovely gowns for dinner."

"Well—"

Gladys whisked her clothes into cabinets and wardrobes, exclaiming over some of them.

None of her clothing was French, and Cora didn't have any tweed, two things that likely encompassed the wardrobe options here. Gladys eventually dressed Cora in her finest gown, murmuring something about how she needed to make a good impression.

Gladys gave her directions to the dining hall, and Cora strode downstairs, armed in her mint satin gown. Unfortunately, the balloon sleeves did seem a trifle outrageous, and the rest of the gown might have had an overabundance of ruffles.

Dining with movie stars was one thing, but it was quite another to dine with English aristocrats greater than twice her age, who had a penchant for narrowing their eyes at her statements. Likely her very accent was cause for amusement.

No matter.

Cora ignored the uncertainty coursing through her.

Voices sounded.

Good.

She must be near the dining room and she rounded the corner of the hallway.

The dining room was nowhere in sight.

Signor Palombi and the duchess were speaking in an alcove, and Cora hesitated.

Are they having a private conversation?

But they've only just met...

She frowned, and some curiosity caused her to halt.

"I don't like seeing you on your own here," Signor Palombi said. "Not with that man. Come with me, Denisa."

He was on a first term basis with the duchess? And he was suggesting she run away with him?

Cora was certain that did not follow etiquette rules.

But the duchess did not seem offended by the man's impertinence.

No slap sounded.

In fact, the space between them was very narrow, and they seemed almost to give each other a hug.

"I can't. I wish I could follow you there," the duchess said. "Spend the rest of my life with you, but I-I have commitments."

Oh.

That sounded *exactly* as if they were having an affair.

Perhaps that was why the duke and duchess had seemed so cantankerous. They were consumed with their own worries, and Veronica should not dwell on their supposed disapproval.

"The child is grown," Signor Palombi said.

The duchess smiled. "He's married, but it feels...wrong."

Cora stepped back. She was not going to eavesdrop further; she'd listened to far too much as it was.

She crept quietly down the corridor until she eventually heard voices, and this time they did not belong to people in the midst of having illicit affairs.

Veronica, her husband, the duke and Lady Audrey were sipping martinis. Beyond them was an elaborately decked dining room table. No doubt they were waiting for the others to arrive.

Thankfully, Lady Audrey was deep in conversation with the duke. She wore a striking black dress that managed to radiate sophistication, if not, precisely, personality. Perhaps she confined her fondness for color to her art.

Cora entered the room.

The duke raised his eyebrows and glowered at her. "Ah, we're only missing four people now. I shouldn't wonder that my children keep requesting money: even the ability to tell time eludes them and their wives."

"I'm here," Lord Holt said quickly.

The duke lowered his bushy brows. "I suppose it's just the ability to make conversation so your presence is known that eludes you."

Lord Holt's cheeks took on a shade of deep rose.

"Were you missing us, Father?" Mr. Ardingley entered the room.

"Just remarking on your tardiness," the duke said.

"We're here now." Mr. Ardingley walked to a bar cart and poured himself a drink as his wife wheeled herself into the room.

She smoothed her forest green gown, running her hands over the drop waist. The sparseness of her thin shoulder straps was not quite hidden by the navy and green shawl draped about her. The lower half of her dress was composed of a variety of ruffles, and beads sparkled from each layer. No doubt the dress had been expensive at one time, but it was dreadfully out of fashion, and worn shoes peeked from the hem.

The duke frowned. "For the amount of time it took, I would have expected your wife to look at least somewhat glamorous."

"She does," Mr. Ardingley said.

"She's been wearing that dress for the past ten years," the duke said. He subjected Mrs. Ardingley to a disdainful stare. "Is that your Christmas dress?"

"I'm sure it hasn't been nearly that long." Mrs. Ardingley raised her chin and kept her voice defiant, but the reddening of her skin, even underneath her substantial powder, impeded the effect. "Besides, I cannot walk. And this is comfortable."

"Comfort is something sought by the weak," the duke replied.

The duchess and Signor Palombi entered the dining room together, and Lord Holt's knuckles tightened around his martini glass. He swallowed the remainder of his drink, and one of the footman scrambled to replace it.

The duchess wore a scarlet gown. The bias cut fabric, and the manner in which the silk hugged her body, made it obvious that unlike other women of her generation, she did not achieve her well-proportioned body through the aid of old-fashioned corsets. Rubies sparkled from her throat and wrists. Her sleeves were not puffed or in any manner billowing; evidently she did not require any volume on her shoulders to create the impression of a dainty waist. The duchess's waist was already slender, despite the cook's undoubted effort over the past thirty years to place temptations before her.

"You look well, Ma," Veronica called out cheerfully.

"She looks beautiful," Signor Palombi said firmly.

"Let's go in," the duke said, choosing not to comment on the Italian's statement. Perhaps he was accustomed to his business partners musing over the attractiveness of his wife.

Signor Palombi offered Cora his arm. "Allow me."

Cora took the man's arm cautiously, pondering whether he was indeed the Duchess of Hawley's lover. They settled around the dining room, and Cora took in the dark paneled walls, adorned with all manner of medieval weapons. Her eyes must have widened, for Mr. Ardingley winked.

She drew back and focused on the less intimidating aspects of the room. Sconces flickered golden light. The ceiling was painted a pale blue color that might have been intended to mimic the sky on a pretty day, since she'd heard that those were rare in England. So far, she hadn't seen a blue sky since Arizona. Even New York had been devoid of them.

Footmen in glossy black attire stood behind them. The frequency of the footmen's glances at her made it clear that they knew her identity.

"It's so quiet in here," Veronica said loudly. "This is a clear case for music."

The duchess frowned, managing to direct centuries of carefully cultivated aristocratic disapproval, but Veronica only laughed.

"You mustn't look so cross," she said. "I promise to not put anything too shocking on."

"We don't own a gramophone," said the duchess.

"Oh, but I do," Veronica said.

"Gramophones are more an indulgence for the servant class," the duke said. "When one has heard the 1812 Overture played at the Royal Albert, one really cannot listen to big band music with all those ghastly brass instruments."

"Unless one is tone deaf." Lady Audrey sipped her glass of wine daintily. "Did I ever mention how truly interesting I thought your Broadway Bonanza of 1936 performance was, Veronica? I could swear your singing voice was much higher pitched in the film. A true soprano. How unexpected when your speaking voice is so deep."

"Men find deep voices appealing," Veronica said. "You may not know that."

Lady Audrey flushed, but she retained a sweet tone. "I merely questioned that you had really used your own voice in the film."

"Obviously the director's taste was questionable. My singing voice is outstanding." Veronica tossed her hair.

Lady Audrey smirked. "Then perhaps you can provide the musical entertainment tonight."

"My gramophone will do quite well. Not all of us listen to music as if we're still scared of the French."

"I'm not scared of any French." The duke pounded his fist against the table.

"We know you're not," said the duchess. "Though perhaps you should be frightened by the Germans."

"Fiddle-faddle," the duke said, momentarily distracted when the footman switched the soup course for fish.

"A gramophone must be an unconventional item to take with you," Mr. Ardingley said. "I think it's splendid you brought one."

"It's for my work," Veronica said. "I'm doing an adaption of *Horror Most Dreadful,* the radio play. I thought I should listen to the original play."

"How thrilling," Mr. Ardingley said. "I've listened to the radio play. Dear Katherine has quite a morbid fascination for the entire crime genre, don't you darling?"

Mrs. Ardingley shifted in her wheel chair. "Only when you place the Proust out of my reach."

Cora had the impression Mrs. Ardingley did not want to enjoy anything that Veronica excelled at.

"So do you have a copy of the radio play with you?" Mr. Ardingley asked. "Perhaps we could listen to that after dinner."

"Oh, how dull," Lady Audrey said. "The most atrocious jazz music would be preferable."

"I agree," Lord Holt said. "Why listen to a version of a play that my darling wife will only perform so much better?"

Veronica beamed and blew him a kiss.

"That is the last moving picture you will be in, I hope," the duke said.

Veronica straightened. "Yes, your grace."

"Dear Father," Mr. Ardingley said. "They don't call them moving pictures anymore. They're no longer a novel concept."

"That doesn't mean they're appropriate," the duke grumbled. No wonder Edmund couldn't bear to introduce this woman to me before his so-called elopement."

"Real elopement," Veronica said. "We're married."

"So you say." The duke took another slurp of red wine, and when he spoke, his teeth were as stained as a recently satiated vampire.

Mr. Ardingley smiled. "You're one to feign propriety, Father. I think you've shocked Miss Clarke with your collection of medieval weapons."

"Good," the duke said. "Those Americans should be scared. Acting like they're the superior power in the world."

"Father is involved in all sorts of mysterious activity with other governments and companies so large they seem entirely devoid of a nation's values with which to adhere."

"Is that so?" Signor Palombi asked. "How exciting. *Fascinamento.*"

"I hope your tongue is not always that loose," the duke said to his oldest son.

Mr. Ardingley flushed.

"So these are medieval?" Cora asked. "I hadn't realized the house was that old."

"Estate," the duchess corrected her. "We don't live in mere houses."

"It's all new," Mr. Ardingley said. "All quite fabricated."

"It's Victorian," the duke said. "You mustn't give the American the wrong impression. They are most gullible."

Mr. Ardingley waved his hand. "This place is fifty years old. Younger than dear father."

"*My* father built it," the duke said.

"It's a monstrosity." Mr. Ardingley took another sip of wine. "One rather wishes our ancestors had started oppressing people in the eighteenth century instead of waiting until the nineteenth, so we could have one of those bright airy places in style then instead."

"Nonsense," the duke said. "Those manor houses look all alike. All dado rails, friezes, and cornices. Ridiculous decorations, as if the English hadn't advanced past appreciation for the Greek column. This is Victorian. This is English."

"I've always liked it," Lord Holt agreed. "I, for one, think Grandfather did a wonderful job building this. It will be my honor to continue the dukedom at this great property.

"Brown-noser." The duke waved his hand, in the same dismissive gesture as his eldest son. Wine spilled from his glass onto the white tablecloth.

Lord Holt's shoulders lowered, as if he were pondering the effectiveness of the centerpieces as spots behind which to hide.

The duchess directed her gaze to Veronica. "Perhaps poor taste runs in the family."

Veronica concentrated on cutting her food, as the room fell into silence except for her knife screeching against the plate.

"Well, I do like this place," Cora said, trying to be polite.

"Your grace," the duke said. "You can call me that."

Cora blinked.

"Father paid big money to get that title," Mr. Ardingley said. "Lloyd George gave it to him in exchange for considerable funds."

"My family's impact on the region was considerable," the duke said.

"Yes, but the impact was hardly good," Mr. Ardingley said. "Anyway, Father is determined to get his money's worth of respect before he dies."

"He didn't mean that, your grace," Mrs. Ardingley said hastily.

"You mean you paid to become a duke?" Signor Palombi asked, his voice incredulous. "How fantastic."

The duke scowled, and his expression did not even improve when the footman exchanged his fish course for game.

"My ancestors made this region great," the duke said. "They provided coal and steel for thousands. The Empire flourished because of the Holt family."

"They lowered the life expectancy of this region to thirty years," Mr. Ardingley said. "But money must be made, and it gave father dearest a dukedom."

"My son is upset that I refused to lend him money," the duke confided. "He is envious he was not as successful as his ancestors. But then he is only my bastard. As I've said before, no bastard of mine will ever inherit a farthing."

Mr. Ardingley stiffened, and Mrs. Ardingley trembled. She wrapped her blue and green shawl more thoroughly around her, as if the cotton threads could offer fortification against her father-in-law's harsh words. Even Lord Holt appeared upset, and Cora wondered how close the two brothers were. Had they played together during holidays? How sad that their futures would have been so different.

Signor Palombi coughed. "Well, your grace, we in Italy are grateful that you can share England's industrial triumphs with us."

"For a price," the duke said hastily. "Always a price."

"*Naturalmento*," Signor Palombi said. "I look forward to our conversation later."

"Hmph." The duke concentrated on his plate.

Cora frowned.

Something about their exchange had felt...wrong.

Obviously, though, everything was wrong. The duke might possess wealth, but his family and business affairs seemed needlessly unhappy. Even the people who did not argue with the duke seemed to be subdued, as if recalling past disagreements with him.

Dinner progressed, and the footmen brought out increasingly complex courses.

Cora sipped her wine. Likely it was complex and to be raved about by wine connoisseurs, but now she longed for something simpler.

"Your dog is very adorable." Cora told Signor Palombi, striving to move the conversation to a more cheerful topic.

The Italian beamed. "*Certo*."

"I like dogs," the duke grumbled. "Bigger dogs. Not your little European petite ones."

Signor Palombi straightened. "Archibald is at the optimal weight for his breed."

"And his breed is suboptimal. White. Fluffy. Not the least bit masculine."

"I find Archibald charming," the duchess said hastily.

"Hmph." The duke sniffed. "Wish you would have let me get a dog."

"You know the reason," the duchess said.

The duke jerked his finger in the direction of Lord Holt. "The boy can't even abide dogs. That's why we don't have any."

"I do not," Lord Holt practically pouted, and Veronica gave Cora an embarrassed smile.

Perhaps children had a tendency to grow less mature in the presence of their parents, no matter how yellow their birth certificates had become.

"What sort of Englishman doesn't like dogs?" the duke mused. "No wonder he married an American."

Veronica's smile wobbled.

"I should have a dog here," the duke continued. "Two hounds. Maybe three."

Lord Holt took a long swallow of wine. "Get some revolting beasts if you want, *Father*."

There was a slight emphasis on the last word, and Cora's eyes narrowed.

No one else seemed to have noticed. What had it meant? Was it possible that the duke was not Lord Holt's father?

Cora shook her head. The thought was ridiculous. Naturally the duke had fathered Mr. Ardingley. Besides, Lord Holt resembled the duke: their noses curved down in the same fashion.

Perhaps nose shapes are not the most effective method of determining paternity.

But then, the duchess had seemed very close to Signor Palombi...

"So you are an actress as well?" the duke asked Cora

"Yes," she replied.

"Ha. I'm not sure when we began to allow such fiddle-faddle into our ranks. Is it true that *anyone* can be an actress in Hollywood?"

"I suppose so, though it is a difficult profession."

She would need to try approaching other studios when she returned.

"It's much coveted," Veronica said. "It's incredibly difficult."

"Ah-ha. So you must have studied at some educational establishment? A dramatic academy?" He sniffed, as if education were something merely for the masses who desired to pretend that by reading about events, they knew something about them.

The duke was actually involved in shaping the world. Veronica had mentioned his frequent excursions abroad, to various sand-covered countries in the Middle East related to some mysterious money matters.

"I never actually studied acting," Cora admitted.

"And your parents approve of you doing this? It seems like such an absurd thing to do. Acting."

"They were the ones who suggested it," Cora said.

"I suppose there are people who would rather pretend to be someone they are not." He gave a definite glance to Veronica, who flushed.

"I warrant her parents always wanted her to be a star," Signor Palombi said. "Some people desire that. They spend so much time with their children and begin to imagine all manner of talents in them."

"It's due to lack of exposure to proper arts and athletic endeavors," Mrs. Ardingley said.

"I never gave Edmund any such encouragement," the duke said.

"Indeed you did not," the duchess concurred. "None whatsoever."

The duke glared at his wife.

"Tell us more about your path to stardom, Miss Clarke," Signor Palombi said.

"It is odd to think back about it," Cora said. "We were living in Vegas at the time—"

"How shocking." Mrs. Ardingley's hand fluttered to her chest.

"My father came back, and he told me he needed me to audition. My mother laughed him off, but he convinced me. Then they drove me to Los Angeles and I did the audition that afternoon."

"And you received the part?" Veronica asked

Cora nodded. "I don't think I had studied that much."

"Then you must be quite gifted," the duke declared.

"Yes," Veronica agreed, somewhat uncertainly. "Indeed."

The rest of the dinner continued to be strained.

"Let's meet in the drawing room for drinks," Lord Holt declared.

Some people murmured agreement, but Cora made her apologies and left.

Dinner had been a brutal affair.

Chapter Five

Cora had no desire to make strained conversation in the drawing room and she headed toward her room. The floorboards might only be fifty years old, but they creaked beneath her, as if warning others of her path.

Or perhaps...perhaps some creaks derived from another person?

Yes.

Someone was following her, and she inched instinctively closer to the wall. She'd experienced sufficient forced chit chat at dinner, and she was not in the mood for further awkwardness. She darted between two marble busts, perched on similarly grand columns. *Thank goodness for art.* The statues must be of Victorian ancestors of the duke: Cora was certain that no Roman god would have been depicted with sideburns and a balding head.

She almost smiled.

If Mr. Bellomo were here, he would have adored to be portrayed in such carefully chiseled stone and would have taken to hiring sculptors instead of actors.

The footsteps sounded nearer, and she shrank farther back. Her back touched the ledge of the window. The glass was icy and wet, and she shivered.

The footsteps continued to patter against the floor, and Cora turned her head. The marble gentleman beside her, despite his significant facial hair, did not succeed entirely in blocking her view.

It was Signor Palombi.

And Archibald.

Well. Cora's shoulders relaxed.

Signor Palombi was at least pleasant.

She was being silly. She couldn't expect to successfully hide her presence.

Given the thick condensation on the windows, she couldn't even claim to be admiring the view. Her lips twitched.

Besides, she wouldn't mind interacting with Archibald. The dog *was* adorable.

She stepped onto the carpet and glanced down the corridor, prepared to greet them.

No one was there.

Where had they gone? The bedrooms weren't on this level. The only room on this floor was the duke's library. Surely Signor Palombi wouldn't have ventured there.

The duke couldn't desire a man he had such contempt for to have access to his private sanctuary and any papers within.

Perhaps Signor Palombi was lost?

Cora approached the library door.

It would be natural to call out his name. But a shiver coursed through her, and she hesitated.

The air in England had felt harsh ever since she'd landed. The icy wind seemed to rush toward her with a never-ending force, whipping against her skin. It wouldn't be long before her skin was dry and weathered. Her hair already felt less silky away from the Californian climate.

But the air in the manor house felt different still. It seemed heavy, as if the statues and paintings, gilded furniture and suits of armor might weigh down on her. Unease prickled through her spine.

Dim light illuminated the hallway, its strength marred by the crystals that adorned the chandeliers. If the crystals were intended to make the light more magnificent, they succeeded only in making it cloudy.

She poked her head through the door.

The room seemed empty, and she frowned.

Could she have imagined Signor Palombi and Archibald's presence?

The room was dark, but she could make out shapes: an armchair, likely leather and luxurious, and a kidney desk that curved on two sides, like Mr. Bellomo's.

She walked past the library door, and it was only when she reached the end of the corridor that she remembered she'd wanted to go to her room.

Voices came from the drawing room, and she was just about to turn around when she heard her name.

"Miss Clarke!" Lord Holt greeted her. "Come join us."

"You can call me Cora," she told him.

For a moment, he looked uneasy, but he soon smiled. "Splendid. And—er—Lord Holt is unnecessarily formal. Edmund will do just fine."

Edmund and his older half-brother were sitting in the drawing room.

"You can call him, Ed," Mr. Ardingley said.

"No!" Edmund said.

"Eddie?" Cora asked, and Mr. Ardingley's eyes twinkled.

A dark rose hue seeped into Edmund's cheeks. "That's—er—not preferable either."

"Don't worry," Cora said.

It was refreshing to be in the presence of someone who was not suave and convinced of the veracity of his every statement.

"Have you seen my wife?" Edmund asked.

"I thought she was planning to join you in the drawing room," Cora said.

"Good."

"Should I go find her?"

"Oh, no," Edmund said hastily. "Don't want to make a big deal about it. Why don't you have a seat?"

Cora hesitated. It would be nice to get to know Veronica's husband better. "Very well."

Perhaps it might distract her from thinking of what exactly Signor Palombi was doing in the duke's library. She had the faint feeling that the proper etiquette might be to mention the fact to one of the hosts. But she'd found the duke so unappealing that she was reluctant to get Signor Palombi into trouble.

She picked up a thick book on the coffee table.

Edmund glanced at the book. "Shakespeare. The only fiction Father permits. Are you a fan?"

"I haven't read much," Cora admitted.

"Oh, that's fine," Mr. Ardingley said. "I don't think Father has either. Otherwise he would be sure to disapprove of all the vile jokes and grizzly deaths."

Cora widened her eyes, and the brothers laughed.

"I don't mean to put you off," Mr. Ardingley said. "It is entertaining, and since you're in England..."

"Perhaps I should read England's greatest author," Cora finished.

"Exactly," Edmund said. "Though you needn't start with Macbeth. Shakespeare would have given a much truer depiction of the British Isle if he'd devoted his life to writing on fox-hunting and degrees of blusteriness."

Cora smiled and flicked to the table of contents, reading titles of plays she'd heard of but never seen. She settled into the armchair. The fire's orange and red flames danced merrily in the fireplace, and she absorbed some of its warmth.

She felt foolish for having desired to retire early. She turned to the first page and began to read. A bone-chilling scream echoed from above, sending a chill down Cora's spine and making her heart stampede against her ribs.

And then a scream sounded.

Chapter Six

The scream soared through the manor house.

It was long.

Fearful.

Cora had never heard the sound of terror so clearly.

But they were alone.

King Kong hadn't wandered into the room.

Cora glanced at Edmund and Mr. Ardingley, as if to confirm the scream had really sounded.

Their eyes were wide, fearful.

"It's Father!" Mr. Ardingley jumped to his feet and rushed from the drawing room.

Edmund and Cora followed him. They hurried up the grand staircase, and Cora cursed the curves in the stairs, which had likely been more designed for beauty than for efficiency.

They sprinted over the carpeted hallway, past carved oak cabinets and painted vases depicting faraway lands. Signor Palombi and the duchess stood outside one of the doors, still attired in their evening wear. Signor Palombi jiggled the door's handle, and Lady Audrey, Mrs. Ardingley and Veronica approached from the other end of the corridor.

"Your grace?" Signor Palombi shouted. "What's going on? Open the door."

The scream continued to sound, but then it stopped abruptly.

A chill swept over Cora.

Edmund brushed past the others.

"Father!" He banged on the door. "Father!"

The room remained silent.

Perhaps it was good.

Perhaps a mouse had appeared, but it had hopped away, and the duke was no longer frightened.

But dread crept along Cora's spine. The duke didn't seem to be the type of person to be unnerved by a mouse, not with his comfort in confronting others, and certainly not with his history of questionable business dealings with foreign powers.

"What's going on?" Mr. Ardingley asked. "Papa?"

"I'll enter via the balcony." Edmund dashed through the next door, which Cora realized must belong to the duchess. They heard another door slam, and then utter silence.

"Edmund!" Veronica shrieked. "Are you all right? How is your father?"

Finally, Edmund swung open the door.

His face was pale and somber.

The duchess pushed past him.

Edmund tried to catch her. "Don't go there—"

"Horace!" screamed the Duchess Denisa, and the others entered the room.

And then Cora gasped.

The curtains were open, as were the French windows leading to the balcony. Moonlight shone over the bed. Shards of crystal and broken glass tubes lay shattered. They glimmered under the strength of the moonlight.

But that was not what drew horror. Horror came from the curve of the blanket that indicated someone was lying underneath, and horror came from the scrapes of dark liquid over white, wrinkled, unmoving flesh.

"Oh, my God," Mrs. Ardingley said.

"My husband," the duchess wailed. "Remove that chandelier. Rescue him!"

She tossed pieces of the chandelier behind her.

Edmund nodded and swept off large pieces of the chandelier to the floor.

"He can't just die," the duchess shrieked. "Not like this."

Unfortunately, it looked horribly like he'd already died. His eyes were glassy and unseeing.

"Do something, someone," demanded the duchess.

"I'll call the doctor." Mr. Ardingley rushed from the room, and the pounding of his footsteps echoed in the corridor.

"Cora, what would you have done in the *Gal Detective* movies?" Veronica asked.

"That's hardly relevant," the duchess wailed.

"She's right," Cora said.

"But there's no doctor," Veronica said. "There's no one else..."

Cora approached the bed and inhaled.

She put her fingers on the duke's pulse. She had done it before in one of *The Gal Detective* movies. There it had been almost amusing, since she'd recited her lines on camera saying that she couldn't feel anything, when in fact the pulse of the actor who had played the corpse had vibrated beneath her fingers.

The duke's wrist was cold beneath her touch, and there was no pulse.

Cora swallowed hard and moved her hand. She brushed some chandelier shards from his heart and tried to listen, but there was nothing, no sound. She was touching somebody who no longer existed.

How quickly death descends.

Cora drew back abruptly. "I'm afraid he's dead."

The wooden floorboards creaked beneath her steps, as if to groan, and she wavered, unsure where she could next step.

"He can't be," insisted the duchess. "He was just alive."

The others stared dumbly at her. Even Signor Palombi's face was white, and he was silent, evidently unable to conjure the power to launch into a speech on the swiftness and finality of death.

Wexley arrived and quickly lit the candles in the room, and Veronica took a candle from him. She resembled a Victorian woman in her gown, and even though Cora knew it was a modern mint, it appeared white under the incessant golden flickers of the candle.

Lady Audrey and Mrs. Ardingley were also wearing clothes better suited for sleep. Mrs. Ardingley wore a long negligee. The polka dotted fabric and pink ruffles on the square shoulder yoke seemed absurdly cheerful. Lady Audrey was clothed in a nightgown, though the long bishop sleeves afforded her some privacy. A lace-trimmed silk eye mask perched on her head.

Cora could tell in the light that even the Duchess of Hawley looked less polished than she'd seemed initially. She was wearing slippers with her evening gown, and her slippers had snow on them.

How odd.

Lady Audrey was silent, and Cora exchanged glances with her.

Neither of them were supposed to be here. They were joint intruders in this family tragedy.

Cora had never even seen a dead person before. Her visit wasn't supposed to start with a blood-spattered host.

Mr. Ardingley soon arrived back, and the butler accompanied him with a flashlight.

"No good, I'm afraid," Mr. Ardingley said. "The lines aren't working."

"Not working?" Cora blinked.

Mrs. Ardingley smiled. "You poor American darling. So unfamiliar with snow."

"And rightfully assuming a proper infrastructure," Signor Palombi said. "England is behind the times."

"Now is not the time to talk about that," admonished the duchess.

"No, of course not," Mr. Ardingley said, his face once again white, as if seeking to match the salty strands in his hair.

"When will the telephone work again?" Cora asked.

"Likely at some point when there is less snow," said the butler.

"Perhaps one of the servants should go into town to fetch the police," the duchess said.

"And someone should remove the body," Veronica said. "It is terribly grizzly."

"Be that as it may," the butler said, "I would prefer to limit the death count to one tonight. I'll send one of the footmen to the village when it's light."

"Of course, Wexley," the duchess said smoothly. "You are clever."

"I say," said Mr. Ardingley. "Is that mustard on your face, Wexley?"

The butler's face reddened, and he removed a handkerchief. "Forgive me. We were having dinner in the kitchen. Cook makes a very good sausage."

"Were all the servants there?" Cora asked.

"Yes. No one misses dinner."

Edmund knelt beside the bed. His voice was solemn. "I can't believe it. It can't be true."

Cora and the others lingered, as if unsure what to do now that their host had been crushed to death.

Chapter Seven

Tree branches rattled against the walls of the manor house, the tapping sound evident despite the howl and whistle of the wind as it thrust through the trees. Snow fell outside, visible through the large windows framed by green velvet drapes that stretched onto the wooden floor, settling into luxurious piles.

The sumptuous surroundings contrasted with the mangled body of the duke. Nausea threatened Cora's throat, and she swallowed hard.

Edmund brushed off the shards of the crystal on the bed, and they slid onto the floor, clanging as they collided with the floorboards.

"I'll send for a maid, your grace." Wexley left the room.

Mrs. Ardingley drew in her breath sharply.

And then Cora realized it.

Your grace.

Edmund was a duke now.

Veronica was a duchess.

All of this now belonged to them, and any tiffs Edmund had had with his father over money were irrelevant. His fortune was large and could not be disputed.

Some aristocrats' possessions did not amount to anything beyond that of their title and property. The latter often acted more as an impediment to the aristocrats as they struggled to maintain their estates and pay governmental fees. Veronica had told her that the duke—the late duke—had not belonged to this category. He'd managed to continue his wealth, investing in weapons during the Great War and unafraid to make deals with other countries to further the interests of his family.

Veronica and she had marveled that the scruffy, determined girl she'd met all those years ago could be transformed into an English aristocrat. She'd seemed to have made good on such a large scale, surpassing even the ostensibly impossible dream of becoming a Hollywood actress. The gossip columnists had marveled over her success and the magnificence of her future title. How had no one contemplated the horrors of death that must accompany any such change in title and fortune?

A maid arrived with a pail. Her face was grim, and she approached the bed with obvious trepidation.

"Please clear the bed as much as you can," the butler said. "The late duke should retain some modicum of dignity."

The maid nodded and placed the pail beside the bed.

Unease coursed through Cora.

Every *Gal Detective* film had mentioned the importance of not disturbing the crime scene.

Of course, this wasn't like those films.

This wasn't a crime scene.

The fact would be absurd.

Except...

The poor man had seemed utterly terrified when he'd screamed.

Perhaps the chandelier had not fallen on him simply because of an accident? Perhaps somebody had been irritated by his constant harangues and had taken matters into his own hands.

"Stop," Cora said abruptly.

Everyone stared at her.

"Why?" Edmund asked. "We can't let him lie under this."

"The police might want to see it," Cora said.

"To declare the death," he said. "Naturally. But he doesn't have to appear so—"

"Undignified," the duchess finished for him.

"A victim of the brutality of chandelier accidents." Mrs. Ardingley smirked.

No one joined her in laughter.

The horror of this could not be overstated.

"But what if his death wasn't accidental?" Cora asked.

Veronica widened her eyes. "Do you think it might be *murder?*"

The word clung to the air, and the others stiffened, their expressions aghast.

"I might be wrong of course," Cora said.

"I assure you that you are," the duchess said. "What possible evidence is there to even suspect a crime? Who would want to kill my husband?"

The silence that followed was of the awkward variety.

Cora had dined with them.

None of them had liked the duke. A great many people did gain from the death, including his duchess. She obviously hadn't cared much for the duke. Devoted wives did not have a habit of bringing their lovers to their home for the holidays.

"I think the police should examine the crime scene," Cora said. "I think it's possible someone dropped the chandelier on him on purpose."

"Then I'll leave my husband's body with remnants of Venetian crystal sticking out of it? I should pay him such disrespect?" The duchess glowered.

"There's nothing we can do for him now," Lady Audrey said.

Likely she was eager to dismiss the tension swirling in the room. Clearly, she was managing to be more effective at it than Cora, for her grace's shoulders relaxed.

"Well, honey. If you think there's a problem, I think it's worth investigating," Veronica said.

"I'm happy to send the maid away," Wexley said, turning a questioning gaze on Edmund, "if you do not have an objection, your grace."

"Of course I have an objection." Edmund scowled at Cora. "What did you mean about the police?"

Cora frowned. "I mean, he died—didn't he?"

"But it was an accident," Mr. Ardingley said. "You can't mean to imply that something untoward occurred."

Edmund nodded and pulled Veronica toward him, and she leaned against his shoulder. For that moment, they looked every bit as wonderful a couple as the gossip columnists proclaimed.

Had it been an accident?

One didn't hear about chandelier deaths.

Could someone have forced it to have come down?

The man had sounded as if he'd *known* what would happen—and feared it.

Was it possible that the scream had occurred before the chandelier crash? Would he have been able to see something?

Could he have screamed so loudly with a chandelier on top of him? *Perhaps.* After all, the man had seemed in control of his vocal chords. He'd certainly been able to berate Veronica and then his own son with every bit of the same efficiency as a much younger Hollywood director.

Edmund seemed to realize the implications and drew in his breath. "I know you are a friend of my wife's, but I do not appreciate that you are in *my house* and standing over my father's lifeless body and insinuating that somebody must have despised him enough to murder him."

Cora's shoulders sank an inch. He was right.

This person had just died, and all Cora had contributed to the alleviation of their grief was pondering whether he had been murdered.

She shouldn't be here.

She should be in LA, where icy wind did not batter against the buildings and where even fires in every room could not mitigate the incessant cold. She wasn't supposed to be pondering investigations. She may have played a detective once, but that had been for the camera.

She could give in.

She could say she was probably wrong.

But what if she wasn't wrong? What if he'd really been murdered? And she'd just walked away? He might have been unpleasant to be around, but no one deserved to be murdered, and no one should go about murdering other people.

"Just who do you mean to suggest may have murdered him?" Edmund asked quickly. "My darling wife? My mother?

The neighbor I've known for years? A renowned businessman? Or one of the servants who have served us loyally?"

"All the servants were in the kitchen," Wexley said quickly.

"Perhaps some murderer ventured in from outside," said the duchess. "Some crazed madman who happened upon my poor husband's room."

Cora's blush deepened.

The idea was ridiculous.

But what if it had it been someone outside? Some madman?

The duke had died in his bed, in his own home, in what he'd been sure to think of as an oasis of comfort.

One rather trusted beds not to become death traps, especially when one had lain in one for multiple decades with no poor occurrences.

"It's good to be safe," Cora said.

Edmund nodded slowly. "Very well. I will lock up the room." He glanced at the maid. "No need to clear the room after all."

The others scattered.

Chapter Eight

Cora's heart beat uncertainly as she exited the duke's bedroom, as if it had forgotten its rhythm in the turmoil. There could be no normalcy after this.

A man was dead.

The concept seemed strange.

She'd just seen him.

The duke had been full of life, despite his wrinkles and propensity to stoop.

The thought that he'd just stopped existing seemed ridiculous.

Yet his death was anything but ridiculous.

It seemed horrible to consider returning and lying down on the soft compilation of velvet coverlets and cotton sheets, ignoring that their host had done just that only to succumb to a violent death.

Had the duke taken in the beauty of his surroundings before he'd gone to bed? Had he admired the rich woodwork on the walls of his room or the shiny porcelain vases decorated with vibrantly colored depictions of Oriental landscapes before he'd gazed at the glittering crystals of the chandelier?

Poor Edmund.

She couldn't imagine what it would be like to lose a parent, especially under such macabre circumstances.

She glanced at the window in the corridor.

The snowflakes' elegant descent to the ground, which had been sufficiently slow so that each snowflake pattern had been distinctly visible, had halted.

Utterly.

Now the snow thudded down, as if some eager worker were shoveling them from the sky. The sparkling, ivory landscape, where snow had adorned every branch, had vanished, replaced by an incessant whirl of white. Moisture fogged the windows, as if even the manor house was telling them not to bother to look out.

Cora retreated to her bedroom and eased onto the four-poster bed. It creaked against her. Updating mattresses was evidently not something prioritized at the manor house, and she glanced uncertainly at the ceiling as if she half-expected to see a chandelier crash down on her.

The ceiling was resolutely bare, and she turned off the single lamp. The room was thrown into darkness, but the house seemed to not have fallen asleep yet.

Creaks sounded, perhaps floorboards expanding and constricting, and the whole place seemed to groan. The wind blustered against the house, and the long branches, bare now of any leaves, tapped against the windows, perhaps warning her to leave, or perhaps as if trying to get in.

Would some madman be sneaking into various rooms now? When the duchess—or would she be the dowager now?—had first suggested that a stranger had done so, it had seemed reassuring that they needn't imagine a person amongst them to have murderous tendencies.

Yet the thought of a stranger being here, perhaps clambering on balconies or crouching in wardrobes, was frightening.

Cora knew the blankets weren't very heavy, but her chest hurt as if weighted by some invisible, yet powerful force.

Her fingers itched against the crocheted blanket that someone had made by hand, likely in the Edwardian Era.

This had not been the calming, peaceful holiday that her friend had told her about.

Home had never seemed so far removed.

Chapter Nine

Something sounded outside Cora's balcony, and she opened her eyes.

Footsteps?

She remembered the murder and clutched her blanket, as if mistaking it for a shield.

Perhaps the murderer was sneaking away...

Or perhaps it was the sound of some local madman...

Cora inhaled, trying to evoke some sense of calm.

She was probably wrong. Weren't there animals in the countryside?

A fox? A deer? Or an owl? Hmm...

Perhaps an owl had jumped off the balcony above to eat some innocent rabbit. Were there rabbits in the winter? She frowned, uncertain. The countryside was a mystery.

Cora moved her hand over her chest, as if to calm her heart.

But it was no use.

She kept hearing the scream, the powerful, brutal scream.

The sound would remain with her for the rest of her life.

It had been a howl, not just of surprise, not just of pain, but of fear.

One would have thought he'd been facing the reaper himself—and that the grim reaper was threatening to use his scythe to dismember him.

Memories of the dead body, of the blood, of the crystal, reflecting like some macabre scene flooded her mind, followed by the unwelcome certainty that someone was outside.

She imagined the person sneaking up to the bed and cutting the chandelier over a sleeping octogenarian until it was too late.

The whole idea seemed absurd.

Yet, wasn't murder something absurd? That life, something so precious yet so taken for granted, could be taken away, not by disease or failure of the heart, but by the simple misfortune of having encountered someone with an evil mind.

The thought of closing her eyes, of sleeping, when there was a chance that someone could be standing on the other side of the balcony door—

No.

She was not remaining here.

No way.

Cora had left her book downstairs. It was likely still splayed open where she'd left it after hearing that horrible scream.

She grabbed her robe and swept it over her nightdress. Her movements were clumsy in the dark, and her legs hit the wall.

No matter.

She hurried down the stairs, reassured that the corridor remained the same as before. The same old-fashioned portraits hung from gilt frames, the people in them staring with aristocratic disapproval. The same ornate mirrors dotted the corridor at intervals, allowing her to see the contrasts between herself and the past ancestors of the Holt family seat.

The modern cut of her satin nightdress seemed flimsy, as if she were missing the frills and pomp of the ancestors of this place.

No one wanted to murder her, she told herself.

She was quite certain that she hadn't insulted anyone irreparably, though Edmund had seemed quite perturbed that she'd dared to suggest his father's death might not be strictly accidental.

She entered the drawing room and turned on the light. The room looked completely innocent, if colder than she remembered. How had she ever managed to think it foreboding? It seemed to possess an innocence she was eager to regain.

She crossed the room and grabbed the Shakespeare volume.

"Can't you sleep, cowgirl?" An amused voice rose from the corner of the room.

Cora froze.

It wasn't the voice of Edmund or Signor Palombi.

It wasn't the voice of either Mr. or Mrs. Ardingley.

Nor was it, of course, the sound of the duchess or Veronica or Lady Audrey.

Perhaps it was a servant who'd taken it upon himself to relax in the drawing room in what she was sure would be termed a flagrant breach of protocol.

Except...

It didn't sound like a servant.

It sounded like someone she'd met.

But it was impossible

It *couldn't* be the person in Veronica's garden.

That had been in Bel Air, and they were nowhere near there.

But he was here.

Thousands of miles away from California.

She thought again of the dowager duchess's comment about strange madmen.

Perhaps the man was a stalker.

Perhaps he adored Veronica and desired her to be even wealthier than before.

Perhaps the next person he would kill would be Edmund.

Or me.

A shiver rushed through her, and she stepped away.

Cora kept her eyes on him, as if he were some tiger on the verge of attack.

Or was eye contact what she wasn't supposed to do?

She frowned, uncertain about appropriate wild animal dodging protocol.

"You're the photographer!" Cora exclaimed finally.

His smile wobbled. "I'm not one, actually."

Cora frowned. Most photographers didn't deny their occupations. She glanced behind him. Something that looked awfully like a camera case, along with a bag, was on the sideboard.

The man was clothed in a not particularly stylish overcoat. The fact did not seem to negate his overall attractiveness.

Sadly.

She was certain this was not a moment for strange butterflies to be coursing through her chest.

Not with a corpse one floor above.

And not when she wasn't exactly sure how this man had gotten in, and who he was, and...

Her breath seemed to quicken, and her legs seemed rather less capable of holding her up than normal.

His eyes filled with sympathy, and he narrowed the gap between them. "I didn't think you would be so taken aback by my presence."

Cora was conscious of the size difference between them.

"But what are you doing here?" Cora sputtered. "You're supposed to be in America."

"My home is in Britain," he said.

"But not this manor house."

"Perhaps not," he admitted. "But you didn't give me a chance to outline my holiday plans."

"You would have told me?"

"If I'd known it involved staying at the same place."

"Who are you?"

"Randolph Hall," he said. "And I believe you're Cora Clarke."

She nodded.

Randolph tucked a strand of hair behind her ear and tilted her face up. His eyes were soft and warm, and he smoothed her no doubt far too frizzy hair. Concern seemed to flicker over his face. "I'm sorry I scared you. Did I wake you up? I tried to be quiet, but..."

She was absolutely certain his voice wasn't supposed to sound so warm and comforting.

She was conscious of broad shoulders and a firm chest.

But perhaps he'd murdered the duke and then been waylaid by the snow. Perhaps he'd already robbed the house, and had been so dazzled by his loot, he'd returned in an optimistic attempt to get more. Or perhaps she was being woefully unfair to him.

He didn't seem like a murderer.

He didn't place his hands in a frightening manner around her collar, nor did he mention any regret that she hadn't decided to put on a scarf.

Tears prickled her eyes, and his eyes widened.

"I didn't want to frighten you." His hands stroked her hair, and he murmured reassurances to her in such a calming voice that she could almost imagine that everything really would be all right.

"You broke in!"

"I wouldn't phrase it quite so bluntly. I did try at the servants' door first, but—"

"No one answered?"

He nodded. "No one expects a visitor at this time of the night."

"That's not the reason," she said.

"Then what is?"

The question was said so casually.

He didn't know.

In his world, it was still unknown that someone had killed someone.

She shook her head. "No. That's not your fault. Not that you should be breaking into manor houses in the middle of the night. It's something else."

"The people here can be so superior. Just because they forced some of their citizens to leave Britain for a better life abroad, they seem to regard all Americans as nothing more than overly cocky peasants."

"It's not that. Though it would have upset me earlier. The duke died," she said.

"What?" His eyes widened. "That's horrible!"

She nodded. It was.

"I suppose... He was an older man, though, and those things are bound to happen."

Cora gave a tight smile, unsure whether to say more.

But it didn't matter.

He was inside the house.

He would learn soon enough.

"A chandelier fell on top of him," she said.

"Truly?" A contemplative expression appeared on his face.

"Yes."

"Well. Dashed older houses."

"Yes." Tears once again threatened Cora's vision. Talking it over with someone, someone who was so kind and caring, was enough for her to relax, and if she relaxed the fortitude with which she was forcing herself to not cry might completely give way.

Chapter Ten

"You should go back to bed," Randolph said. "It's the middle of the night."

"I should say the same to you."

"I'm not supposed to be here," he reminded her.

"Nevertheless, you're here now. I doubt you want to return to the snow."

"I wouldn't be able to make it out. I had to abandon my car. There were huge snow drifts every which way. I don't remember a winter so bad."

"Are you from here?" Cora asked

"No, lassie. I'm from Inverness, the very top of the world and a top place to be. A much more sensible location with more trucks that took a speedy view of the need to discard snow. I'll just sleep on a chair here. Or," Randolph said, his lips moving into a roguish grin, "you could offer me space on your bed. I assure you I am quite good at keeping chandeliers off people."

Cora flushed.

Veronica would laugh if she saw her now. Cora had a vague idea that another woman might bat her eyelashes and perhaps even smooth the lint—or in his case rapidly melting snowflakes—from his coat.

But that was not to be.

A creak sounded in the hallway, and Cora stiffened.

Probably nothing.

Weren't the floorboards of houses supposed to be forever expanding and constricting, as if the trees were still fighting the indignity of having had their bark stripped from them, and being cut into thin slivers of their once majestic selves?

But the noise continued, and Cora recognized the plodding rhythm of careful footsteps.

The door moved open, and Cora's breath quickened, and—

It was the butler, in his impeccable black uniform, and she released her breath.

"Miss Clarke." He gave Cora a placid nod, but his serene expression soon wavered. His eyebrows seemed to have had the urge to take flight, for they soared upward. "You have a gentleman caller."

The word may have been gentleman, but if he had said the word devil, he could not have had more disdain on his face.

Cora suddenly felt utterly improper and wanton.

Cora was a young woman alone with a young man in the middle of the night.

And she wasn't even clothed in proper attire.

"I was not aware that you had brought a guest, Miss Clarke." Disapproval dripped from his words, with the effectiveness of kindling on a fire. "I am unfamiliar with what strange customs you might have in California, but I can assure you that in this household, the door is only answered by me, no matter your romantic urges."

"I am afraid you misunderstood. This young lady—er—Miss Clarke happened upon me in the living room." Randolph moved away from her.

"I did not let you in," the butler said.

"I found another method," Randolph declared with nonchalance. "No one answered my knock on the front door. I entered through the French doors." He leaned closer to Wexley. "You will, I am afraid, need to repair those."

The butler's face took on a purple tint. "I cannot permit you to break and enter—"

"It was cold outside," Randolph said.

"Then you are an utter stranger, descending on this house in the middle of the night?" The butler kept his gaze on Randolph, but he stepped backward slightly and stretched a gloved hand to one of the large brass candlesticks.

Tension soared through the room.

The butler clutched the candlestick and swept it before him. The occasional strand of gray in the butler's hair did not hamper his fitness.

"The Duke of Hawley invited me," Randolph said. "Miss Clarke just told me that he has passed away. I am so sorry."

Cora blinked.

Randolph hadn't mentioned he'd been invited.

The words had an immediate effect on the butler, and suspicion eased from his face. "Still, the duke did not mention other visitors..."

Surprise seemed to flicker over Randolph's countenance, and Cora wondered whether he might, in fact, have belonged to one of the swarms of handsome men who descended on Hollywood with regularity, hoping to transform any gift of deceiving others into a monetary value.

"But perhaps he wouldn't have mentioned it," Randolph said. "I was supposed to arrive tomorrow, but I hoped to beat the storm. I tried to call, but—"

"The lines are down," the butler said.

"My car didn't quite make it. The snowdrifts were rather excessively sized."

"You probably drove your car over next years' roses," Wexley said, his voice mournful.

"Look, let me give me you my card." Randolph shuffled through his pockets and then removed a business card triumphantly.

The butler took it skeptically and held it to the light. "Randolph Hall, Private Detective."

Cora inhaled sharply.

Was that why he had been hiding under Veronica's hibiscus?

He wasn't a photographer at all?

But he was, perhaps, far more dangerous?

Why on earth would the duke have hired a private detective to investigate Veronica?

And why would he have followed her all the way here?

Wexley tapped his fingers against Randolph's business card. "Detective? What is this about?"

"The duke was adamant that he needed to speak with me in person." His tone was suave, and perhaps it reassured the butler.

Wexley sighed. "I suppose you'll need to speak with the young duke. Given the snowstorm, I cannot turn you out. Follow me. One body on these premises is enough."

Chapter Eleven

Sunbeams flooded Cora's room, and she blinked into the bright light.

"Oh good, miss. You woke up." Gladys smiled at her from the window. "I hope you don't mind me drawing the curtains."

"Not at all, Gladys."

It took Cora a moment to remember that her host had died, and another yet to remember Randolph's mysterious appearance.

Gladys handed Cora a cup of tea, which she accepted gratefully. She downed a lengthy swallow of the hot drink and set to work on the rest. If only British tea were as strong as American coffee. No wonder the duke had spent his lifetime complaining; it was likely inevitable while drinking such weak liquid.

"I heard the duke was killed. How gruesome!" Gladys's tone was almost cheerful, as one might discuss a particularly bad impending storm when one had neither farmland nor property about which to worry.

"It's true," Cora said.

"You poor thing," she said. "Lady Audrey said you were one of the first to see the body."

Cora nodded. "Lord Holt...er, His Grace and I came up from the parlor together when we heard the scream."

"So terribly frightening," Gladys said, but her eyes glistened even more than they had when she'd quizzed Cora about her experience in pictures. "I suppose you'll need to wear black clothes. Do you have any? The village shops are closed for Christmas, and of course, with this snow, you'd have to ski there."

"I don't ski," Cora said. "But I do have one black dress—"

"Ah." Gladys opened the wardrobe and evidently found it. She held it out triumphantly before her. "Here it is."

The black cocktail dress had seemed overly conservative in Hollywood. The sleeves didn't billow in an interesting manner, and there was no large satin ribbon in the front that Cora could tie into an exuberant bow. But now the material seemed too shiny, and the hem seemed too short. It was intended more for cocktails than breakfast, but it would have to do.

Gladys helped Cora into the dress, even though that seemed unnecessary. The dress was rather lacking in buttons and ties to make dressing her a two-person endeavor. Cora had never once failed to successfully put on her normal clothes, and she thought it unlikely she would begin now. She'd never felt an inclination to wear a corset, like some members from the older generations.

Gladys frowned. "It is rather short."

"I think I might have brought some black stockings..."

"Good thing it's the old duke who's dead. He's the one who would have criticized you."

"Gladys!"

The maid shrugged. "It's true."

"Perhaps," Cora admitted. "Though you mustn't speak ill of him. It may not have been an accident."

Gladys widened her eyes. "How exciting! Just like in the pictures. You could call it *The Case of the Dead Duke.*"

"If only it were a film."

Gladys rummaged through the chest of drawers and picked up the black stockings.

After Cora's attire looked reasonably somber, Gladys gave her directions to the conservatory, where the others would be taking breakfast.

Cora strode through dark wood paneled corridors until she reached a cheerful room with large windows. The wind roared, and the glass panes seemed too delicate to serve as any sort of barrier.

Cora reminded herself that the manor house had been standing for decades and it was likely it could overcome any unconventional wind patterns.

It might be the height of winter, but potted plants were neatly lined up, and Cora inhaled their pleasing scents.

Perhaps the room was a haven from the cold, but she wasn't certain it was also a breakfast room.

When she rounded the corner, the others were sitting stiffly around a table covered with various breads and cheeses and some other items of shades of yellow and red that likely comprised the English breakfast.

"Miss Clarke. Sit beside me," the duchess said.

Cora nodded and settled into a wicker chair that seemed better suited for summer. She glanced at her breakfast companion.

Carefully coiffed auburn curls lay elegantly over the duchess's head. She'd changed into an ebony colored dress. Perhaps the shine in the taffeta material was not strictly mourning appropriate, but the manner in which it rustled seemed definitely old worldly. Perhaps her husband had died, but she'd not seen any necessity to diminish the elegance of her attire.

At least not with Signor Palombi here.

The duchess met Cora's gaze. "Wexley informed me that a strange man is sleeping in one of my guest rooms."

Oh.

"I happened upon him in the drawing room," Cora said. "He said your husband had invited him."

"What? Horace did that?" The dowager duchess's voice broke. "My late husband was not prone to including me in business relationships."

"A good thing, my dear," Signor Palombi said hastily. "His ties were not always appropriate."

Cora tore her roll and spread butter on it, wondering if the Italian would mention more. Veronica had also referred to the late duke's deeds in an opaque, though decidedly negative, fashion.

"Perhaps this strange man's some enemy of Father's who murdered him and then, when the snow impeded his escape, decided to reenter the house," Mrs. Ardingley mused.

"How horrible!" Veronica gasped.

"Wexley should have ushered him out." Mrs. Ardingley said.

"It was snowing awfully hard, and it was the middle of the night," Cora said. "Besides, he mentioned he was a private detective. He had a business card."

"Anyone can call themselves a PI," Mr. Ardingley said.

"I had met him before," Cora said.

"Truly?" Veronica laughed. "When did you manage to do that? I thought we were always together in this country."

"I didn't meet him in this country."

"Surely he's not the Scotsman under thehibiscus?" Veronica smiled, as if certain the answer would be no.

Cora lowered her gaze, and Veronica's face whitened.

"At least I can vouch that he's not an ax murderer or anything like that," Cora said.

"You can do no such thing, my dear," the duchess said. "Just because you met a person on one occasion, and he did not take out a shining piece of sharpened metal and start brandishing it about like some medieval maniac transported from the past, does not mean he will not do it on another occasion."

"He's apparently handsome," Veronica said.

The duchess frowned. "And a man's possession of handsomeness does not signify a possession of honesty. In fact, I have found there can be a distinct negative correlation between a man's looks and the veracity of his words." She gave a pointed look at her son. "Naturally, the same applies for women."

Veronica flushed, and Edmund's eyes narrowed. "Just what are you implying, Mother?"

The dowager duchess gave an innocent smile. "Merely that this strange guest may be the mad man I was warning you about. Or did my comment remind you of anything else?" She glanced at Veronica again. "There were no strangers here, but one has appeared. *Voila.* Now if only Wexley can get the telephone working, we can get Scotland Yard to whisk him away in whatever hideous vehicle they drive about in."

The others laughed, but Cora was silent.

She hadn't trusted Randolph when she'd first seen him. Why was she doing so now? The dowager was correct. He had been outside in the middle of the night.

Perhaps she should have woken up everyone in the house when she'd encountered him in the drawing room.

"At least the police should be able to clear this up," Veronica said.

Wexley cleared his throat. "There is still a problem with the phone, your grace."

"You mean no one is coming from the police?" Veronica asked. "But there's a body!"

"Not a body. My husband. Yes, he is lying there, but he will keep. The coldness will see to that." The dowager frowned. "I hope the maids will not light the fire in the bedroom."

"The maids can be quite willing to watch the most macabre things in the cinema," Wexley said with a pained expression, "but that delight does not extend toward actual corpses."

"Sounds like an excuse not to clean the room," Mrs. Ardingley said. "Sloth is a sin. Let's leave this place soon, Rhys."

"I think it is perhaps wise if no one leaves," Cora said. "The police might want to interview you."

Veronica sniffed. "You have far too much faith in the police, my dear. You do remember Constable Kirby? It will just be an utter bother and waste of time."

"Exactly," Signor Palombi said, twirling his mustache. "How tragic that the country's greatest detective—Sherlock Holmes—never actually existed."

Mr. Ardingley yawned. "The girl has a point. Let the police come. We've got nothing to hide. If there is a mad man terrorizing this region, we should at least let them investigate."

"Yes, yes," the duchess waved dismissively and bracelets jangled from her wrists. "How am I supposed to believe," Lady Denisa continued, "that this man truly came to meet with my late husband? Perhaps he's some horrid journalist. You wouldn't believe the number of people who knocked on this door after the elopement."

"We cannot throw him out of here," Veronica said. "Not in this weather. I wouldn't like to imagine what he would write about us then."

"Christmas is next week," Lady Denisa said. "It's the period renowned for people denying entry into their homes, no matter the emergency."

"Mother, that was *not* the moral of the Christmas story." Edmund rolled his eyes in obvious exasperation. "If Veronica believes we could create worse problems by not hosting him, I have no inclination to do that. We have plenty of rooms in this manor house. We don't need to have anyone freezing to death on our conscience."

"This is a tiresome conversation," Mr. Ardingley said. "Shouldn't we have mimosas for breakfast? I find that a delightful tradition that we should emulate."

"Most people consider champagne a festive drink," Lady Denisa said. "I'm certain your father's death does not count as a celebratory occasion."

"Don't be too sure," Mr. Ardingley murmured.

"There are some drinks in the bar, Rhys," Edmund said.

"I know where they are," Mr. Ardingley grumbled. "This was my father's place too."

There was an awkward silence while Mr. Ardingley poured whisky into a glass.

Lady Denisa turned toward Cora. "Perhaps you're the murderer."

"Me?" The word came out too similarly to a laugh.

"Indeed." Lady Denisa's voice was icy, as if the cold weather had affected more than the outside of the manor house.

"But I just met him," Cora stammered.

"You are American." Lady Denisa flinched slightly as she said the word, in the same manner that others might refer to communists or fascists. "Do not Americans adore violence?"

"Nonsense," Cora said. "No one likes violence."

"Perhaps." Lady Denisa's voice was calm. "But Veronica told me you were in a Western. Isn't that one of those films where you wear suede and shoot up desert towns?"

"We are not in a desert, Mother," Edmund said.

"Oh, but she might still be feeling the urge to see violence. That's probably why she insisted my dear husband was murdered. You were in detective films, weren't you? Probably piqued your interest in murder."

"Those films were confined to missing jewels and secret passageways," Veronica said, rather unhelpfully.

"I only met your husband yesterday," Cora said.

"That would suffice in inspiring lesser mortals to begin serial murder careers," Mrs. Ardingley said blithely.

"That's absurd," Cora sputtered.

Lady Denisa frowned. "It's no more absurd than suggesting that someone he knew, someone he trusted, had killed him. Someone like—"

"You?" Cora finished. "Forgive me."

Lady Denisa retained a pained expression on her face.

"Besides Mother, I was with Miss Clarke when Father screamed," Edmund said. "It couldn't have been her. American or not."

"Oh." Lady Denisa sighed. "I forgot."

Her shoulders slouched.

"It's fine," Cora said, uncomfortably.

The dowager duchess shouldn't have looked so distressed at the thought Cora was not a murderer.

Or is there someone else she thinks committed the crime?

"I think one question is," Lady Audrey asked, "why did the late duke hire a private detective? Who's got something to hide?"

Chapter Twelve

"FOR AN ARTIST YOU ARE revoltingly scandal free," Mr. Ardingley said, addressing Lady Audrey. "You just had the unfortunate bad luck to accept my little brother's invitation to come here for Christmas."

Lady Audrey glanced out the window. "Well, I was right that it would be pretty at least."

"I know why Father hired one," Mr. Ardingley said.

"Indeed?" Lady Denisa asked.

"He's been complaining about Edmund's rash elopement for months. I suspect he put a private detective on your new wife. Miss Clarke did say she saw him in America."

Oh, no.

Veronica's face became stony.

"Was your new wife too racy for Father, brother dear?" Mr. Ardingley's eyes sparkled.

Edmund's face pinkened. "That can't be the reason. Veronica is—er—positively angelic."

"You're not going to tell me that she was a virgin." Mr. Ardingley laughed again and downed the amber-colored liquid in his crystal tumbler. He marched to the bar.

"Considering that it's morning, I think you've had enough." Mrs. Ardingley pursed her lips. "Otherwise you won't remember anything."

"And why would that be bad?" Mr. Ardingley swung around, and his eyes blazed with a strange ferocity. "My father died," Mr. Ardingley reminded them, as if they might possibly have forgotten. "Why on earth would I want to linger on that memory?"

"Calm down," Edmund said. "It was just an accident."

"Oh, you're in denial," Mr. Ardingley said. "It's murder."

"Because a former starlet says so? Someone who played a detective for the silver screen?" Mrs. Ardingley lifted her eyebrow to a lofty level. Walking might pose difficulties for her, but she obviously excelled in eyebrow movement. "I would hardly take her opinion seriously, Rhys dear. I'm not even sure Miss Clarke finished high school."

"I did!" Cora exclaimed.

"Is that so?" Mrs. Ardingley's eyebrow did not move downward.

"Yes," Cora stammered. "With—er—tutors."

Mrs. Ardingley gave a smug smile. "Hardly the same thing though."

"Let's find out what your wife did," Mr. Ardingley said. "Or just tell us now, Veronica."

Veronica's face whitened, but she only laughed. "Obviously it was nothing."

"Don't lie to me," Mr. Ardingley said. "I'm not in the mood."

Edmund rose. "Come, Rhys. We know your mood doesn't extend to anything nonalcoholic now."

Mr. Ardingley frowned. He picked up his newly refilled glass and flung it onto the ground. It shattered into many pieces, and the scent of whisky permeated the room.

"Happy, brother?" Mr. Ardingley drawled. He turned to the others. "Shall we go to the library? I know where Father stores his files."

"Stored," Edmund said.

Mr. Ardingley flushed. "Er—yes."

"Let's go read them," Mr. Ardingley said he added cheerfully. "Perhaps you have a crime record."

"I don't have a crime record," Veronica insisted. "Anything in there would be lies!"

"I think you're lying," Mr. Ardingley said.

"Well, not a current one. Not as an adult."

"You've only been an adult for two years," Mr. Ardingley pointed out. "Two years without a record is hardly a great occasion for celebration."

Veronica's smile wobbled. "Perhaps I should have some of that whisky, Rhys."

"No one is drinking anymore," Edmund said sternly. "Perhaps Father was hoping to find something. But that didn't mean he did. And now it doesn't matter, because he's dead."

Veronica smiled. "Thank you, dear."

"Perhaps you murdered him," suggested the dowager duchess.

"Mother!" Edmund widened his eyes. "Please don't accuse my new wife."

"I heard what your father had found out about her," the dowager duchess said. "He wanted to expose her."

"Expose what?" Mr. Ardingley said.

The dowager duchess shrugged. "Oh, just that she lived on the streets for a while. When she was twelve. And eleven. And I believe also when she was ten. Three years in total. Who knows what could have happened then? Not exactly the proper background for a duchess."

Veronica gritted her teeth together. "That's a lie."

"I don't think so, dear. I read the reports too."

"But—" Mr. Ardingley stammered. "How—? Why—?"

"Well, I imagine she had no choice," said the dowager. "That is rather what happens if you're homeless. As for how... I believe it involved some singing on the streets. Some dancing. Not very decent at all."

"It wasn't three whole years," Veronica said slowly. "And I had a roof over my head—mostly. And I worked. I entertained people."

The dowager duchess shrugged. "Clearly your life has improved. Though I think it would be good to destroy whatever documents Horace had. You might want to also see if you can pay off that inspector. I've never much cared for scandals, and I really don't have the patience for them at my advanced age."

"But how did you manage to recover from that?" Lady Audrey asked.

"It's not important," Edmund said quickly.

"But it seems impressive," Mrs. Ardingley said. "I must admit to being curious too."

Edmund raked his hand through his hair. "She doesn't want to talk about it."

"Look. I entered a beauty queen competition. First prize was a screen test for Hollywood. And I won. That's all. Utterly uninteresting."

"And the criminal record?"

"Was for stealing clothes from a local department store," the dowager duchess said.

"It worked," Veronica said. "I had to look nice and I did."

"That's amazing," Cora breathed.

The others seemed similarly awed.

Veronica shrugged. "It was the start of this dreadful depression. You had to do what you had to do."

"Still. It's a motive for murder. Father wanted to destroy you for having the gall to marry into the family," Mr. Ardingley said. "I imagine the new *duchess* wouldn't want that sort of thing to get out now."

The mood was broken.

"I thought we were friends, Rhys," Veronica said.

"My father died. And apparently somebody killed him. That matters to me."

"I didn't do it," she said softly.

"Where were you when he died?" he asked.

"In my room."

"Did anyone see you?"

Veronica shook her head.

"I think the police are likely to see you as the most likely suspect too."

"But I didn't—"

"So you said." Mr. Ardingley rose and left the room.

"I'll follow him," Mrs. Ardingley moved her hands to her wheelchair.

"I'll send a footman to assist you up the stairs," Wexley said.

Mrs. Ardingley nodded.

Murmurs of excuses to go drifted through the room, and it soon emptied.

Cora swallowed hard.

If only she hadn't informed every one of her suspicions that it was a murder.

Now her dearest friend was in trouble, and it was all her fault.

She reminded herself that the police would sort everything out.

Perhaps the village constable didn't exude competence, but that didn't mean he couldn't solve the case.

Except he'd likely never had to investigate a murder. The village didn't seem large enough to have them often.

And he's not even here.

Perhaps Cora could discover who the murderer was herself. She would need to speak with Edmund. He knew everyone more than Veronica did, and perhaps she would be able to discover other motives.

They needed to speak in private.

Cora found Edmund in the drawing room with Lady Audrey.

"I believe the snow has finished, Edmund," Cora said. "Would you perhaps show me around outside?"

Edmund blinked.

"I mean, there's nothing else to do now."

"Shakespeare is not that interesting?" He sighed. "I suppose I could show you the barn. We have some skis and snowshoes there."

"Splendid," she said.

She was not going to spend the day inside, not when there was a chance she could help Veronica and make sure that the duke's murderer would not remain free.

"Would you like me to join you?" Lady Audrey asked. "Edmund is not the best skier."

"No need," Cora said quickly.

"Well, do enjoy yourselves."

Cora followed Edmund to the foyer, and a footman brought them their winter garments.

Chapter Thirteen

Cora's relief at not having Lady Audrey with them soon gave way to discomfort. Edmund's demeanor met all the minimums for politeness, but he made no attempt at friendliness.

She followed Edmund outside, and frigid wind prickled her skin. "It's cold."

"Indeed."

Cora had met other gentleman callers of Veronica's of course. Most of them had been movie stars, though some had gained entry to the finest establishments because of their bulging bank accounts, rather than because of any talent or even because of the good looks that so often substituted for talent in Hollywood. She missed their cocky enthusiasm for the future and gleeful embrace of the present.

Though she had known there would be snow-covered fields and had even looked forward to them, the cold had seemed an abstract concept. In Los Angeles, a chilly day had meant a sweater. It certainly hadn't meant three sweaters, an overcoat, some excellent boots, thick socks, and a woolen hat would still make her feel underdressed and cold and miserable.

Edmund led the way to the barn. The snow drifts were not as large on this side of the manor house, though her boots sank nearly all the way through the snow, and the flat stone barn on the next hill seemed unimaginably distant.

"Tell me more about your father," Cora said.

"You met him."

"I didn't have the pleasure of his company for very long."

"No."

"You must miss him," she said.

"It hasn't been that long." Edmund lengthened his strides over the snow.

"I suppose that's true." Cora scrambled after him, her breath coming out in smoky puffs. "Do you spend much time in the country?"

"I try to avoid it," Edmund said. "Mayfair exceeds this place in charm."

"But you made an exception."

"Yes. Everyone goes home for Christmastime, and Lord knows this is pleasant enough, if one can avoid the people inside."

"Whom would you want to avoid?"

He frowned, and warmth cascaded over Cora's cheeks, despite the air's frigidity.

"If you were your *father*, whom would you have wanted to avoid?"

"Are you asking me whom do I think killed my father?"

"Hypothetically."

"I think it was an accident," he said.

"Tell me more about your mother. Was she close to your father? I mean, obviously they had you—" Cora gave an awkward laugh, but the tips of Edmund's lips plunged into a deeper frown.

"They were no different than any married couple," Edmund said stiffly.

"She's not English, is she?"

"She's from Czechoslovakia," Edmund said. "At least that's what it's called now."

Cora did not inquire whether he referred to the country's comparable youth or whether he was hinting that Germans might, as some feared, invade it.

"How did she and your father meet?" Cora asked.

"In London."

"Why did they marry?"

"He probably thought she was pretty. He was rich, and he liked that she was the daughter of a count." He smirked. "Though in the end he outranked his father-in-law."

"And why did she marry him?"

Edmund frowned. "Would you prefer to be going on a walk with my mother?"

"Er—no," Cora said quickly. "I was simply making conversation. Not very good conversation, I'm afraid."

He nodded. "Likely that's because you're used to someone giving you scripts to read out loud in advance."

"Er—yes." Cora's face warmed. No doubt it was the color of one of Veronica's more dramatic lipsticks. "What sort of business activities was your father involved in?"

"My brother Rhys would say unsavory ones."

"And you would say?"

"Well, he helped people. If somebody wanted something, even something their governments might not be allowed to let them do, Father would find a way to assist them."

"Oh," Cora said, not entirely understanding.

"I suppose it's possible that someone outside might have been angry with Father," Edmund mused.

"What had he been working on?"

"He met mostly with Germans this decade. They're upset that they're not allowed to develop their army as much as they would like, but fortunately Father was able to cut through some of that international red tape. He helped them in the past work out ways to manufacture different parts at different factories so that no regulators grew suspicious. He's quite open-minded, after all. He did marry a Central European. And obviously what is the point of developing one's army if other countries are only going to complain and build theirs stronger?"

"He arranged this with favorable interest rates for himself, I imagine?"

"Naturally." Edmund beamed. "He was very clever."

"I can see that some others might feel differently."

"Yes. People are prone to grumble when they see Germans rebuilding their army, even though Hitler has assured people multiple times that he just desires peace. It's all simple prejudice of course. The last king was far more favorable to Germans. More enlightened."

"Was that the king who was never crowned?"

"Yes," Edmund said curtly. "A tainted past is not something Englishmen can forgive."

Cora jerked her head toward him. What did Edmund make of Veronica? She might not have been a divorcée, but Veronica's scandalous past must cause the man pain.

"Quite a few of your countrymen are helping Germany," Edmund said, changing the conversation to the more neutral topic of arms transactions. "Some people will always make money in arms production. Why not my father?"

"And is Signor Palombi involved in these business dealings?"

"Yes."

"Would he have had a reason to be upset with your father?"

"Nonsense." Edmund pushed open a door of the barn. "Signor Palombi is Italian. Italians are quite accepting of the German desire to secure their position. Mussolini is an ally."

Cora half imagined that they would be confronted by a row of hungry looking horses and cows, but she followed Edmund into a small room. The livestock must be on the other side, and instead there were neatly lined up snowshoes, skis, and skates. On the other side of the wall was summer athletic equipment: a boat, some actual badminton and tennis rackets, not the type that went on feet, and variously shaped balls for all manner of activities that she was sure included plenty of unknown rules.

Edmund took her cursory exclamations of wonder with the disinterest Cora's murmurs probably deserved. "Do you want to use anything?"

The idea of strapping something that resembled tennis rackets onto her feet was not the most appealing of suggestions, especially when a murderer might be on the loose.

"Oh, perhaps not," Cora said.

"You just wanted to see them?" He raised an eyebrow.

"Yes." Cora scrutinized them. "They—er—look similar to the American sort. I—er—just wanted to check."

"Then I will return to the manor house," Edmund said.

"I'll come with you," Cora said quickly.

Upon reentering the manor house, she considered the fact that there had been no great revelations.

"I'll see if I can find Veronica," Edmund said.

"Of course," Cora said quickly, and she was almost relieved when he went up the stairs.

Footsteps approached her. "It's the cowgirl."

Cora turned toward the man's voice.

Randolph stood at the entrance to the foyer, munching on a roll.

The light flickered from the stained-glass windows ahead, giving him an angelic appearance that Cora hoped very much he deserved.

"You're seeming very quiet," he said, narrowing the distance between them.

"Sorry," she said quickly. "It's the murder. It's—"

"Upsetting?"

"Indeed."

"Just leave it be," he said. "Enjoy England. Perhaps we can take a walk together?"

It would be easy to give in.

But she knew so little about him and so shook her head. "I'm just going to enjoy my time here."

"No investigating?"

"Naturally not," she said, feigning affront. "That would be foolish. And besides, perhaps the duke wasn't even murdered after all."

"That's not what you said last night."

"Last night I was sleepy," she said. "My mind is clearer now. More—"

"Well-teaed?"

She tossed her hair. "I'll just go upstairs."

"So early in the day?"

"Yes," she said and ascended the steps before he could ask her more questions.

She wouldn't be able to find out anything if she spent time on walks with him, likely marveling at the splendor of the icy gables and turrets of the manor house.

She moved over the corridor, glancing at the paintings and sculptures that decorated it.

"Miss Clarke," Mrs. Ardingley called out, and Cora jumped. "You are wandering the upstairs alone. Did going outdoors with my brother-in-law exhaust you so much you felt compelled to take a nap? I didn't know he was such a fast skier."

"We didn't do any skiing." Cora shifted her legs over the carpet, absentmindedly noticing the thick pile and wondering if Mrs. Ardingley found the multitude of carpets irritating.

"Yet you still desire a nap?" Mrs. Ardingley smirked.

"I-I was actually hoping to see the maid."

It was the first excuse she thought of, but it seemed absolutely the wrong thing to say. Mrs. Ardingley's expression shifted at once

"Such concern for fashion," Mrs. Ardingley said, and Cora knew she didn't mean the words as a compliment. "You should ask her to press your black clothes and remind her to do your hair in a style with some sobriety."

Cora touched her hair, conscious of her loose locks.

"Curls are not somber," Mrs. Ardingley said firmly. She set her teeth into a thin line, and her hands moved to the sides of her wheelchair. In the next moment, she rolled away.

Cora remembered to be polite and hastened after her. "I could help you."

Mrs. Ardingley turned her head sharply. "Of course. You can do *many* things, can't you?"

Cora's cheeks warmed.

"Acting and walking," Mrs. Ardingley continued. "Though I heard lately you haven't been good at the former, even though you've been doing it for all your life."

Heat continued to spread over Cora's face.

"Don't mind me," Mrs. Ardingley said. "No one does. I'm an invalid. I can be ignored."

"I don't want to ignore you."

Mrs. Ardingley's lips sneered, and other actors might be impressed with the malice she displayed. "You do."

The wheels rattled over the hardwood floors, and Mrs. Ardingley was hardly impeded by the occasional Oriental carpet, presumably priceless, that dotted the floors. Mrs. Ardingley might be in a wheelchair, but she was strong.

Strong enough to kill someone.

"Where were you when the late duke died?" Cora asked.

Mrs. Ardingley smirked. "I suppose I should feel flattered that you think I could have anything to do with the murder." She gestured to the wheelchair. "This keeps me away from following any impulse to murder people."

"How long have you been in the chair?"

"Since Easter."

"I'm sorry."

"So am I." She shrugged. "Not that I was the best match for him anyway."

"You're in the same circles as him."

"That's not what I meant."

Mrs. Ardingley fixed accusing eyes on Cora. "And you shouldn't pretend you don't know what I mean."

Cora needed to change the subject.

She did know.

Of course she knew.

It was obvious to anyone, even if Cora's time in Hollywood would have made her more conscious.

Mrs. Ardingley's nose was too large, and her chin too defined. Her brows were bushy, something she could have changed with relative ease, but perhaps she'd given up on any attempt to mimic basic fashion. Her hair was thick, but rather than appearing luxurious, the strands seemed frizzy.

"He thought I had money," Mrs. Ardingley said. "A reasonable assumption. But then twenty-nine happened, and I lost the use of my bank accounts."

"I'm sorry."

Mrs. Ardingley shrugged. "I shouldn't complain. It's less of a struggle than any of the village boys went through in the last war. But Rhys expected more. I don't blame him."

"He told me he was the first born son of his father."

"He would have made a delightful duke," Mrs. Ardingley said. "So good at galas."

"Do you think anyone wanted your father-in-law dead?" Cora asked.

Mrs. Ardingley pursed her lips together and for a moment Cora thought she might leave all together. "No, naturally not. At least..."

"At least?"

"Most of my father-in-law's enemies tended to be somewhat abstract. Corporations. Governments. Not people. But your friend had a reason. I find her a more likely killer. Edmund and Veronica's room was near the duke's. They had a lovely view of the garden. It would have been easier for her to slip in there than anyone else. Of course Signor Palombi is a stranger too, but why would an Italian businessman want to kill someone who supported Italy's chief ally?"

"Did you hear your father-in-law scream?"

"My ears aren't gone yet," Mrs. Ardingley said. "I did."

"And then you—"

"I stayed in my room. It's not like I could do anything," she stressed.

"Were you alone?"

She glanced at her watch and tucked the blanket that covered her legs more firmly about her. "I was alone. Rhys was in the drawing room, I believe."

"He was," Cora confirmed.

Could Mrs. Ardingley have made a chandelier come down?

Cora sighed.

No.

Chapter Fourteen

"Hello, ladies." Signor Palombi waved to Cora and Mrs. Ardingley from the other side of the hallway.

Mrs. Ardingley frowned. "It's that beastly Italian. And his dog."

Archibald raced toward them, wagging his tail with as much eagerness as he moved his legs. He stopped before the wheelchair

"One of the few good qualities of this place was always the lack of a dog running about and spreading all manner of germs," Mrs. Ardingley said, placing her hands on the wheels. "Go away! Shoo!"

Archibald's tail did not cease wagging, and he sniffed about Mrs. Archibald's feet.

"Dogs seem either terrified or delighted with my chair," Mrs. Ardingley said, her voice strained. "I'm afraid Archibald belongs to the latter quality of beasts. Far too curious."

"Archibald!" Signor Palombi said. "Come back."

Archibald continued to lick Mrs. Ardingley's legs, and for a moment, it seemed that her leg moved.

Cora blinked.

That couldn't be right.

"Well, I should be going." Mrs. Ardingley put her hands on her wheels and rolled away quickly.

Cora stared after her. Was it possible Mrs. Ardingley had the use of her legs after all? But why would she be in a chair? She'd had the impression that Mrs. Ardingley was paralyzed.

"Miss Clarke," Signor Palombi said. "I see you do not share Mrs. Ardingley's unease with dogs."

"She was tired."

"I appreciate the attempt at a lie. The English can be trying, no?"

"But there are many people here who are not English," Cora said.

"Yes, you are American," Signor Palombi said.

"And you are Italian."

Some expression Cora couldn't place flitted across the man's face, but he soon gave a cocky smile. "*Certo*. Though..." He paused, and Cora found herself leaning forward. "Archibald is English."

The dog tilted his head upward, as if unsure about the veracity of the signore's statement.

"He is adorable," Cora said. "Amidst all this uncertainty."

Signor Palombi's eyes softened. "Would you like to hold him?"

"Oh, I suppose—"

Signor Palombi scooped Archibald up and placed him in Cora's arms.

Cora stroked Archibald's fur. The curly white locks felt silky beneath her touch, and Archibald gave her his paw.

Cora shook Archibald's paw, noting the leathery texture.

"His nails need clipped," Signor Palombi said apologetically. "I've been traveling."

"A nice trip?" Cora asked.

"Indeed."

"Which part of Italy are you from?" Cora asked.

"Are you very familiar with the country?"

"I've never been there."

Though Pop is from there.

"I'm from the pretty part," the Italian said. "Vineyards and ocean. *Multo bellissimo.*"

"Tuscany?" Cora ventured.

He beamed. *"Exactimento."*

She blinked.

Her father had said *esattamente* or sometimes just *esatto.*

But perhaps the Italian language had simply changed since her father had last been there.

"I hope you were able to conduct some of your discussions with the duke before his death."

"The trip was not entirely worthless."

"What is the exact nature of your business?"

"Imports, exports."

"Weapons?"

The word hung in the air, and Signor Palombi frowned. "What makes you ask that?"

"Just a hunch."

"Those can be dangerous, young lady."

"I was simply curious," she said.

"Hmph. Death does make one contemplative."

"It is horrible what happened." She assessed the man's face. Would she find a flicker of guilt?

But the man simply frowned and fixed a stern stare on Cora. "Any death is tragic. But it would be perhaps a mistake to assume that all deaths are *equally* tragic."

"No one should die before their time."

"I agree," he said, his voice firmer than she would have imagined. He had not seemed to espouse a desire for justice for the late duke. "But accidents happen, do they not? I assume you've dropped something in the past. Even if you're still very much in your youth."

"Well—"

"Perhaps you've even heard something fall before, when no one dismantled it and crushed it into the space below."

Cora's cheeks flamed. "Naturally. Where were you when you heard the duke's scream?"

"What a curious question."

"We Americans aren't known for being subtle," she said.

Signor Palombi's lips twitched. "No, you are not. I was in my room. You saw me when you came up the stairs, did you not?"

"Yes," Cora said.

"I suppose you want to know if I killed him."

"Did you?"

"That was meant to be a rhetorical question." He shrugged. "You Americans really are not subtle."

"I did warn you," Cora said.

He smiled. "So you did. No, I did not kill the duke. I had only just met him."

It was tempting to make an excuse to leave, but Cora refused to do so.

Not when asking Signor Palombi questions might help Veronica.

"How was your business meeting with him?"

"We hadn't had it yet."

"Why were you in his library shortly before his murder?"

He was silent.

This time she did see a flicker of emotion cross his face.

It was of guilt *and* fear.

He raised his chin though. "I was going to meet him there."

A door opened behind Cora, and Signor Palombi grabbed Archibald.

"I shouldn't keep you." Signor Palombi strolled away from Cora quickly. She turned around and saw him enter his room. Whoever had opened the door had disappeared, and Cora frowned.

Who except Signor Palombi would be in his room? The maid?

Cora hesitated for a moment, but no sound came from behind the thick wooden doors.

Not that I should be eavesdropping.

This wasn't one of the *Gal Detective* films.

Cora wrapped her arms around herself.

The one thing she was certain of was that Signor Palombi was not what he seemed.

Chapter Fifteen

"Miss Clarke!" A voice bellowed across the corridor, and the dowager duchess strode into view.

Her auburn hair was partially obscured by her veil, which extended to cover her face.

"I heard you interrogated my son," said the dowager duchess.

"He showed me the barn."

"Apparently you asked him many questions."

"Just conversation, your grace."

"I do not appreciate it. That boy does not understand how easy it is for him to get into the papers."

Cora glanced at the other doors. Who might be listening behind one of them?

"Perhaps we should talk in a more private setting."

"Very well, Miss Clarke." The dowager duchess marched into a small sewing room off the corridor, with Cora following behind, and then sat down. Her back remained rigid, as if she wore an old-fashioned corset, despite the fact that even the most traditional women's magazines had likely long since ceased advocating their use.

She exuded elegance.

Cora sat on a chair opposite.

Somehow, Cora had assumed she would know what to say. One could hardly begin a conversation by asking a woman if she'd happened to murder her husband. Some things were not appropriate, no matter what class one belonged to, and undoubtedly the duchess had a refined knowledge of what questions belonged to the strictures of decorum.

Last night the action might have caused the duchess to arch an eyebrow, but at the moment her eyebrows remained in place. Her eyes seemed vacant, as if they were not seeing Cora, but perhaps reliving happening upon the scene of her husband's death.

The dowager was the first to break the silence. "Who did my son think was guilty?"

"He didn't know."

The dowager duchess sniffed. "Well, Edmund never was the intelligent sort. Or the athletic sort or even the partying sort for that matter. It's obvious who killed him."

"It wasn't Veronica. She barely knew him."

"You should have heard the way my late husband spoke about her. She would have been clever to hasten the end of his life if she wanted to remain married to Edmund."

"I assure you that Veronica is no murderess."

The dowager duchess sighed. "Perhaps. Though you should feel sorry for my son. He got entrapped by that horrid actress."

"If you could just detail the events of last night. Perhaps you remember something that might be helpful."

"That's the sort of question a constable might ask."

"Then consider it practice."

The dowager duchess shrugged. "It really was all terribly dull. Horace was arguing and making a dreadful fool of himself all through dinner. It was quite unpleasant."

"Was that unusual?"

"No, though it had become rare for him to have the opportunity to act unpleasantly before so many people at once."

"Did you go straight to bed after dinner?"

"Yes."

"And how was the duke's mood?"

"Bad." The dowager shrugged. "Not that that was unusual."

"Did you see or hear anything last night?" Cora asked.

"No." The dowager duchess frowned.

"But you were in the room beside him. Surely you must have—"

"I didn't," said the dowager.

"Did you go outside? Perhaps on your balcony?"

The dowager duchess's eyes drifted to the side. "Of course not."

"It's just—" Cora wavered, wondering how much she should say. She was supposed to nod and act demurely. She was fairly certain she was not even supposed to venture into the duchess's room, lest the dowager duchess miss some stitches on her embroidery.

But it didn't matter.

She was not some debutante, anxious to win the duchess's approval.

She was an American, and the sort already presumed to possess poor habits.

"Your grace," Cora said, more determinedly. "I saw snow on your slippers."

She was glad she'd faced the dowager, noting how her eyes widened.

The action could not have taken more than a second, before the duchess resumed her look of casual nonchalance. She sipped her tea, seeming to savor it, even though it must have been placed in the room following breakfast, long enough for the temperature to fall to an unpleasantly cool degree, and long enough for the milk to taste worrisomely unappealing.

"You must have been mistaken," the dowager said.

"I was not," Cora said. "I was an actress. My memory is excellent."

"I see." The dowager took another lengthy sip. The china clattered when she returned the cup to the saucer. "I do remember. I was outside. But it was inconsequential."

"Why were you outside?"

"I desired some fresh air."

"In the courtyard?"

"Nonsense. Simply my balcony."

Cora nodded, as if the information were indeed inconsequential, but she hadn't realized that the duchess and the duke shared a balcony. She could have slipped in and murdered him. Perhaps she'd done so.

"Your balcony extends to the late duke's room."

The dowager sniffed. "I assure you I did not sneak to his room like some besotted ingénue, intent on being deflowered to be able to boast about my sophistication to the other girls. I knew the duke. Heavens, I married that man. There was nothing to be besotted about."

"And angry about?"

The dowager lowered her gaze and took another lengthy sip of her tea. "We had a good marriage. A proper marriage."

"A happy one?"

The dowager duchess sighed and gestured about the room. "Do you see anything here to be unhappy about?"

The marble busts and gilt-framed portraits seemed to stare back.

Everything was perfect.

"I thought not," said the dowager with a condescending smile. "You Americans value money."

"But did you love your husband?" Cora asked.

"Darling, does anyone love their husband?" This time the mirth that danced in the dowager's eyes was unmistakable. "This is life, my dear. Not whatever fanciful notion you know from some script. He made me wealthy. He gave me a healthy son and provided for him. I was content. I'd be a fool not to be." The duchess frowned. "Do you know what life was like in Czechoslovakia? Do you know what life is even like there now?"

"Did you have an argument with the duke last night?"

"He was my husband. Naturally we did."

"What did you argue about?"

She sighed. "I thought he was too harsh on Edmund. The boy never cared for dogs. No reason to humiliate him. Horace was distressed at the whims of the younger generation. He thought Edmund's bride utterly unsuitable."

"I see. But you thought otherwise?"

"She's horrid. One only had to take a cursory glance at her to determine that she was far too young and famous for him. And her past! It was a great torment that our son did not have the good taste or analytical capability to recognize it. But perhaps there are some benefits to the marriage. He can start with the business of procuring an heir and some spares. At least Veronica's features are pleasing, even if her heritage is no better than any of the chamber maids."

"What did you think about your husband's business affairs?"

"They're none of my concern."

"You mentioned that you came from Czechoslovakia."

"I've been living in England for decades."

"Yet do you have an opinion on your husband's eagerness to capitalize on Germany's desire to rearm itself? That must be worrisome for you."

"Miss Clarke." The dowager duchess inhaled sharply. "Horace is my late husband, and I cannot comment on any of his business dealings. It would not be appropriate for me to do so in any case."

"And what about personal matters?" Cora asked.

"I don't understand."

"Were you having an affair?"

The dowager duchess pressed her lips into a firm line. "That is none of your business. Not that anyone would have blamed me."

"You seemed to be very cozy with Signor Palombi."

"Nonsense." She met Cora's gaze defiantly, but the dowager duchess's shocked tone seemed forced.

"Did you know him before?"

"Signor Palombi? Naturally not." The dowager's skin grew pink.

"And the balcony—would it be possible for any other person to access it? Is not his room beside yours?"

"I won't tolerate this interrogation."

"I'm only trying to have a better idea of what happened."

"Whatever happened did not involve Signor Palombi. Of that I am absolutely certain."

Cora blinked.

The dowager duchess's answer was very firm.

"What was your opinion on Mr. Ardingley and his wife?"

"Oh." Her grace's shoulders relaxed somewhat, as if relieved to no longer be questioned about the Italian businessman. "Rhys has always been much like his father. Far too arrogant for his own good."

"And his wife?"

The dowager shrugged. "It's a pity about the chair. There was one time when I thought they would be quite suited together."

"Not anymore?"

"I imagine Rhys consoles himself about his wife's poor health and even poorer temper in all sorts of biblically unapproved manners. Now, excuse me. Perhaps you are not tired, but I am."

The dowager duchess swept past her and exited the room. Nothing about her gait seemed slow or unsteady. Indeed, she seemed bequeathed with bountiful supplies of energy.

Perhaps she would have been able to murder her husband. Could she have entered the duke's bed through the balcony, locked his door, climbed onto the duke's bed when he was sleeping, unscrewed the chandelier and dropped it on her husband? Could she then have hurried back into her room through the balcony and then feigned surprise and grief with everyone else?

Cora sank back into the armchair. The snow continued to cascade down, and the flames leaped in the hearth.

Perhaps all the Europeans cowered to her, but Cora was not going to take the dowager duchess's statement as truth. Heaving a sigh, Cora departed the duchess's sewing room.

Chapter Sixteen

"Heavens." Veronica widened her eyes as Cora stepped into the corridor. "What on earth were you doing in the dowager duchess's room?"

"I thought she might be able to give a clearer picture on the late duke and who may have murdered him."

"Hmph." Veronica frowned. "Simply because your father is Catholic does not mean you should feel compelled to imitate a martyr. One would think that looking at all those gruesome crosses with blood practically dripping off that poor man's wounds would suffice."

"She's your mother-in-law," Cora said. "I'm hardly burning myself at the stake like Joan of Arc."

"It couldn't have been a pleasant experience, though."

"No," Cora agreed. "You know, she quite reminds me of you."

"Impossible."

"Pretty and very determined."

Veronica gave her a tight smile and paced the corridor. Energy seemed to rush through her. Finally, she halted. "I really must apologize. This is not the quiet countryside holiday I imagined for us."

"Well, it *is* quiet."

Veronica shrugged. "Come to my room. Edmund doesn't like me smoking in the corridor."

Cora followed her into a large bedroom. Dark wooden paneling lined the walls, and Oriental carpets covered the floor.

"It's rather grand, isn't it?" Veronica asked.

Cora nodded, still taking in the damask curtains that seemed to have been made with gold thread, and the elaborate mirrors with frames that appeared gold-plated.

Veronica took out a thin cigarette and placed it onto her cigarette holder. "Goodness. I don't know whether to be eager for the police to arrive or not."

Her hand wobbled, and Cora narrowed her eyes.

Nervousness had never been one of Veronica's traits. Not when she had such an abundance of self-confidence.

"They're going to think I did it," Veronica said.

"Nonsense."

"You heard them at breakfast. Even Rhys thinks so, and I always got along well with him." Tension didn't ease from Veronica's features, and her jaw seemed to stiffen in a manner one might associate more with the eponymous character from Tchaikovsky's most famous ballet than with Hollywood actresses.

"I've never known you to worry about things," Cora said.

"This isn't a small thing."

"But you don't have a motive."

Veronica gave her a strained smile. "I would have hated for any of my horrid past to come out. Just the thought of it now being released makes me nearly swoon."

"You didn't know he was looking for reasons to annul the marriage."

"You're too sweet, Cora. But I did know. I did worry about it. I didn't kill him, but I could have. I was there in that hallway.

Maybe people will believe that I entered his room—nobody ever locks them, lest they decide to call for a servant—and unhooked that chandelier and killed him."

"And exited from the balcony? That's nonsense."

"I could have exited from the duchess's room. I heard her laughing and cavorting with that Italian fellow. I knew she was in that room."

Oh.

"If you heard, other people did," Cora speculated.

"Perhaps it was Lady Audrey. Perhaps the duke insulted her painting."

"Perhaps," Cora said, though they both knew that Lady Audrey and the duke had seemed to get on well, and that Lady Audrey stood to make no financial gain from the man's death.

"It's hopeless," Veronica said. "The village would be happy to have me be the chief suspect. They'd hardly want to imagine that someone they *knew* had done it. And who wants to have one's relative arrested? Something like that would cast a shadow over future birthdays and holiday gatherings. One moment one is reminiscing about someone, and the next moment one's remembering that the person in question spent his last moments on earth dangling from a noose." She sighed. "The servants were all eating when the murder took place. None of them left the kitchen then. Somebody can attest to it for all of them. Not that any of them would have left. The cook's food is delicious, especially around the holidays, and leftovers are not a concept that I imagine the servants are aware of."

"We don't get leftovers either," Cora said.

"No, not with these formal dinners." Veronica giggled. "We could always sneak into the larder if we get too hungry. I just wish the tabloids hadn't delighted so much in smearing my reputation. The wedding was supposed to make me more respectable, and instead the journalists seem to delight in contrasting me in the most negative way to my so very proper husband."

Cora didn't mention that Veronica's past was rather more scandalous than even the most determined journalists had discovered. "Police officers don't read tabloids."

"I wouldn't be too sure," Veronica said. "And they definitely watch movies. Honey, they've probably seen me be arrested half a dozen times by tough coppers or gumshoes on the silver screen."

"At least Constable Kirby is unaware of your repertoire."

Veronica's lips twitched.

For a moment, all seemed well, and Veronica settled against the window seat. "I think I should have gone outside with Edmund and you. This house is giving me the creeps." She peered through the window. "Honey, is that that funny Italian? Why is he carrying such a huge knapsack?"

"What do you mean?" Cora followed Veronica's glance.

And swallowed hard.

Signor Palombi was skiing away from the manor house.

He's fleeing.

Chapter Seventeen

Cora rushed from the room.

"Where are you going?" Veronica called after her.

"I'll explain later," Cora said over her shoulder.

She raced down the stairs, sliding a hand along the polished banister.

It all made sense.

Mr. Palombi had come to kill the duke.

Or perhaps he'd intended to steal some documents, something from his library, and the duke had found out.

She threw her coat on and slid on her other winter garments.

If only it weren't winter and going outside didn't involve such complexity. She sprinted from the house and gazed into the distance at Signor Palombi's receding form.

"Signore!" she shouted. "Signor Palombi!"

If he heard her, he didn't answer.

But then it was unlikely his last name was even Palombi. No true Italian would make so many mistakes with the Italian language.

Skis.

If she skied, she could reach him.

Or at least, she'd have a better chance of reaching him.

Her feet crunched against the snow as she raced to the barn where Edmund had shown her the skis.The bitter wind slammed against her face, but she didn't hesitate. This was her chance. Her one chance.

Would anyone believe her if she expressed her doubts about Palombi's authenticity? Would he go off to murder other people?

She wasn't going to take that chance.

Cora stormed into the barn and grabbed the skis. They seemed long and unwieldy.

Never mind.

She had the basic idea.

Even children skied.

Surely she could too.

Cora changed into some ski shoes, carried the skis onto the snow, and put them on.

She slid her right ski, and then her left ski on the snow.

Her movements were nowhere near as quick as Signor Palombi's, but she was moving.

She was skiing.

She was doing it.

Just as if she'd done it all her life.

Well, perhaps not *exactly* the same, because then she was quite sure she would be going much more quickly, and she definitely would not be looking at the approaching downward slope with terror.

Still, there was something pleasant about the breeze against her face, and she quickened her pace.

Signor Palombi was still visible before her, and she was thankful he was lumbered with a heavy backpack. Archibald's furry white face peeked out; what did he make of Signor Palombi speeding over the snow?

Signor Palombi moved each leg outward, as if he were ice skating, and his skis crossed in a perfect pattern over each other.

Cora attempted the same move, but despite the abundance of dance classes she'd taken, it only resulted in her right ski firmly keeping her left ski in place.

She almost toppled.

She should have toppled.

But Signor Palombi turned around, and Cora managed to stay upright, even though every inch of her body seemed to desire to swerve toward the ground.

For a moment, she thought she saw him smile.

She decided to just keep her skis straight.

That should work better.

Hopefully.

She hurried toward Signor Palombi, focusing on his ever-diminishing figure when—

She skied over the incline of the hill.

She'd done so before of course.

But the slope of this hill was steeper, and she moved downward at an utterly unwelcome speed.

This was dreadful.

She'd never moved so quickly.

She was flying down the hill, and she realized that pointing her skis straight downward was perhaps not helpful in slowing the speed.

She tried to think.

Had she seen skiers before on the newsreels?

Had they done something else?

She seemed to remember that they'd moved from side to side, and she veered toward her left and—

She fell.

On her bottom.

Not that that prevented her from keeping sliding down the hill, unfortunately.

Her left ski came undone and toppled downward, and her right ski decided to stay firmly in place so as to best humiliate her when she tried to scramble after the other one.

Cora grasped hold of her poles and coaxed them into the snow, as if they were the only thing to keep her steady.

She supposed they were.

"What on earth are you doing?" A voice bellowed behind her.

Randolph.

She jerked her head to the side and toppled farther into the icy white powder.

"Cora!" He rushed over the snow, not sinking into it, as if he were some Biblical persona.

Not that Yorkshire could be the least bit confused with the desert settings of those stories.

"Are you hurt?" Randolph kneeled beside her and stroked her hair.

Cora pulled herself up. "You're wearing snowshoes!"

"Er—yes. But my question remains—"

"I'm fine. It's Signor Palombi," Cora stammered. "He's getting away. He's the murderer!"

"How do you know?"

"He's escaping! He's guilty. And I saw him sneak into the duke's library last night. I followed him there."

Randolph turned to her sharply. "You shouldn't have done that. You could have hurt yourself. You could have injured yourself now."

"Snow is soft," Cora grumbled.

"The slopes are steep, and frankly, you don't know what you're doing." Randolph's face darkened.

"He's not even Italian."

"What?" Randolph widened his eyes.

"He's just pretending. I think he figured out that I knew—and I told him I knew he'd broken into the duke's library, and now he's getting away and now he's going, and my best friend in the entire world might hang and—"

Randolph's gaze softened.

"Don't worry." Randolph stood up and offered Cora his hand. "I won't let him get away. Give me your skis. Now."

"But—"

Randolph scrambled to the ground and undid his show shoes. "Wear these."

Cora nodded and bent to remove her remaining ski. Randolph sighed and picked up the one that had fallen off. At last, she stepped onto the snow, unconstrained by those odd Nordic contraptions.

"I need your boots too," he said.

"What?"

"To wear with the skis."

"Oh." Cora undid them.

Randolph tore off his scarf and placed it on the ground. "Step onto this."

"You won't fit into my shoes."

Randolph grinned, and his green eyes sparkled, like grass on a dewy day. They seemed so lively, and it seemed impossible that he might fail.

He pulled out a knife, and the blade gleamed under the sun.

Who carries a knife with them?

"Former scout," he said. "Important to keep it sharpened."

Randolph sliced through the heel of the boots, shoved his feet through them, and then wrapped string around them.

"You always carry that?" she asked.

"The scouts trained us well." Randolph grabbed hold of the poles, and then he was off, pushing himself forcefully down the slope.

Golly.

Cora stared at his receding figure. He seemed a paragon of strength, unfazed by the ever-increasing rapidity of his speed down the hill. On the contrary, he bent his knees and tucked his poles up, so the metal ends pointed into the air, to increase his pace even more.

The man seemed oblivious to the fact he might be headed into danger.

Cora wouldn't let him do it alone.

Not when she was the one who'd sent him there.

She slipped her feet into his boots.

They were far too large.

She frowned, but then shoved her mittens into the space behind her ankle.

Better.

She tied the boots and then put on the snowshoes.

They seemed absurd. Utterly unwieldy, but when she began walking, she appreciated that she didn't sink into the drifts. She forced her bare hands into her pockets and quickened her pace, watching as Randolph pursued Signor Palombi.

Randolph's athleticism should not have been surprising.

His broad chest and shirt sleeves that barely disguised the rippled curves of musculature should have been warnings, as were the confident strides he took that highlighted his powerful form.

Still, his speed was incredible. He scurried down the incline, and for a moment, she didn't see him, but she soon saw first his hat, and then the dark curls underneath, and finally his coat and legs as he tackled the next hill. He ascended it quickly, as if unconstrained by the skis, seeming to go every bit as fast as he would if there were no snow here and he were merely running. He moved each ski diagonally to the side and evidently, the manner in which his skis crisscrossed, which unlike hers never actually touched, seemed sufficient to keep him from sliding down the hill.

"Signor Palombi!" Randolph hollered. "Stop!"

Signor Palombi was not stopping.

The man must hear Randolph. Cora had no difficulty hearing him, even though she was much farther away.

Finally Randolph closed in and—

He grabbed the man.

Relief coursed through Cora.

Randolph was strong, and Signor Palombi was burdened with an awkwardly sized bag. Perhaps, just perhaps, everything would be fine.

Cora padded over the snow in the snowshoes. She tried to emulate perfect confidence and calm as best as she could when her coat was splattered with very cold and very wet material.

A scarf covered nearly Signor Palombi's entire face, but it was him.

"Let me see you," Randolph said.

His voice was all triumphant, and Cora beamed.

They'd caught the murderer.

Once the police arrived, they could haul him away.

Safety was once again restored.

Signor Palombi unwound his scarf and lowered his hood.

Randolph stared at him. "It's you."

"Yes," Signor Palombi said.

"What are you doing here?"

Signor Palombi's eyes drifted to Cora. "Holiday. An—er—important one."

Randolph frowned. "This man is not the murderer."

"But—" Cora blinked. "He snuck into the man's library and—"

"It appears suspicious," Signor Palombi said amiably.

"*Most* suspicious," she said.

She'd thought Randolph would help her.

She'd thought she'd found the murderer.

"I don't understand," she said.

Randolph's eyes softened. "I'm sorry."

"Let me just say that certain people were interested in the late duke's business dealings," Signor Palombi said. "War is in the air, whether the British government desires appeasement or not. Some people think it is useful to know what the Germans might have planned."

"You wanted plans for weapons? Designs?" Cora asked. "You're a spy?"

"He's not going to confirm that," Randolph said quickly.

"I didn't murder the duke," Signor Palombi said.

Cora frowned. "I think that's for the police to determine. You should still come back." She turned to Randolph. "Are you a spy too?"

"Nonsense," Randolph said breezily.

"But then who else would have murdered the duke?"

The two men looked at each other.

"I think I should inspect the body," Randolph said finally. "It may not be murder, and Mr.—"

"You can go on calling me Palombi," the fake Italian said.

"Mr. Palombi," Randolph continued, "will just become the scapegoat if he leaves now."

"I can stay a bit longer," Mr. Palombi said after a pause. "I have grown fond of the manor house and its inhabitants."

They turned back toward the manor house, as confusion continued to course through Cora.

Chapter Eighteen

Randolph and Signor Palombi skied slowly beside her. The gray stone of the manor house rose forebodingly over the crisp white snow, casting shadows over the icy moat. The leaves had been stripped from the trees, and gnarly branches stretched outside the manor house, as if to offer further protection.

"I'll go inside," Signor Palombi said.

"Good idea," Randolph replied.

Cora gazed at the duke's window. Just as the dowager had admitted, the balcony outside extended to her room. But it was also connected to a third room. Siignor Palombi could have accessed the duke's room via the balcony.

"When did you visit your bedroom?"

"After dinner. At—er—ten o'clock."

"After you had a chance to look through the duke's things?"

He nodded. "I heard somebody outside the door and decided not to stay for long."

"You heard me," Cora said.

He nodded gravely. "After that I went straight to my room."

"When did the duchess arrive?"

He flushed. "She was already there."

Randolph raised his eyebrows. Evidently, he did not know Signor Palombi as much as he claimed.

"Did you hear anything?" Cora asked.

He shook his head. "No."

"Did you leave your chamber at all?"

"No! Not until I heard the duke scream." He looked at Randolph. "It was a terrifying noise. It was of someone who truly feared death. And now I will go inside. If I am to stay here, I will at least make certain that dear Archibald is fed."

He marched into the house.

"It was brave of you to go after him," Randolph said. "But also incredibly foolish."

"I wanted to protect my friend."

"Let me look at the body. I have some experience in these matters, and I don't want you to get hurt." He glanced at the snow-filled road. "Besides I think we'll be here for a while."

Cora's lips twitched. "It's possible."

She directed her attention back to the duke's window. A large tree sat outside. A few stubborn leaves fluttered on the tree's dark, spidery branches. They drooped downward, as if regretting their insistent perch and contemplating the soft bed of snow beneath them.

Had someone climbed up this tree to the duke's room? The branches were slick with frost, and they didn't seem sturdy enough to hold someone. But perhaps she was wrong.

If only she'd devoted time to tree climbing as a child. The strength of tree trunks and branches had never seemed of particular interest before, but now it seemed of the utmost importance. She scrutinized the diameter of the branches. Perhaps the murderer had gone to that branch, and then the one diagonally over it, and then—

"You think someone may have climbed up the tree to enter the duke's bedroom?" Randolph asked.

Cora jerked her head toward him.

Perhaps he was also capable of climbing onto trees, and not just crawling beneath them.

"That tree wouldn't hold an adult," Randolph said, with an air of authority. "Besides I don't see any footprints underneath it."

"It was snowing all night," she said.

"Perhaps," Randolph said, "though that doesn't change the fact that the tree wouldn't hold anyone."

She nodded. Perhaps she should yield to his expertise.

Something didn't feel right, but Randolph tucked a lock of hair behind her ear.

"It's windy," she said apologetically.

His gaze was more serious. "You have beautiful hair."

Heat flooded her cheeks. "It's too dark. And it doesn't hold a curl well."

"It's thick and silky," Randolph said. "And the color is beautiful."

She turned away. Her heart pattered in her chest. All talk of trees was forgotten. She couldn't talk about climbing trees. Not when Randolph's eyes seemed to gaze at her in wonder. Not when she longed to tuck herself against his broad shoulders as protection against the world.

"You don't have to investigate this," Randolph said. "That's not your job."

"Someone died. He didn't want that either."

They reentered the manor house, and a servant came to assist them in removing their winter outerwear.

"I'll get the key to the room," Randolph whispered. "Meet me up there in ten minutes."

Voices sounded from the drawing room, but Cora ascended the steps. Perhaps they might investigate while the others were otherwise occupied.

Perhaps she could see if all the rooms on the corridor were occupied. The dowager duchess's room might have been on one side of the duke, but who was on the other? Maybe the duke's room had not shared a balcony with that room, but was there perhaps an adjoining door?

She decided to enter the room in question.

Cora opened the door.

It was another bedroom, and someone was inside.

Mrs. Ardingley.

Except she was...standing.

Cora swallowed hard.

Mrs. Ardingley didn't stand.

She was in a wheelchair.

"Who's there?" Mrs. Ardingley jerked her head in the direction of Cora.

Instinctively Cora stepped behind the door. She pressed her back against the wall, and her heart hammered.

The picture rail dug into her spine, and she glanced at the stairs.

Perhaps Mrs. Ardingley hadn't seen her.

Perhaps if she walked on the carpet, Mrs. Ardingley wouldn't hear her footsteps and she might escape.

Because if Mrs. Ardingley could stand, if she could walk—perhaps she'd had the capability to murder the duke after all.

Why on earth was she keeping her ability to walk secret? If Cora had been confined to a chair for a period and then recovered, she would be taking every chance to walk.

Did her husband know?

"Miss Clarke," Mrs. Ardingley called out, and Cora stiffened.

A shiver, not attributable to the lack of central heating, swept through her.

Should she flee?

"I know you're there," Mrs. Ardingley said.

It was no use. Mrs. Ardingley had seen her. They were confined to a manor house. Cora could hardly succeed at spending the entirety of the time avoiding her.

Cora stepped from behind the door.

Mrs. Ardingley had settled back into the chair.

It didn't matter.

Cora had seen her walking, and Mrs. Ardingley's reliably icy composure seemed ruffled.

Cora glanced around the room. For the first time she thought those men in westerns might have a point when they didn't appear without a pistol. Candlesticks stood on a nearby table. Perhaps she might protect herself with one of those?

Faint clinking sounded, and she moved her gaze upward.

A crystal chandelier hung above them, and Cora straightened her back. The clear glass reflected all manner of colors.

Things are not what they seem.

How could material devoid of any color under the right circumstances seem in possession of every color? Had someone devoid of any appearance of means killed the duke after all?

Mrs. Ardingley laughed. The sound was bitter, halting, as if she was unaccustomed to the action.

"I'm not going to dismantle the chandelier and fling it at you, if that's what you're worried about."

Cora flushed.

"You Americans," Mrs. Ardingley said. "You really are too fanciful."

Cora gritted her teeth. "You can walk."

Mrs. Ardingley flushed, but then raised her chin. "It's of no concern of yours."

"You told everyone you couldn't. Everyone thinks you're lame."

"Well. I'm not."

"But why would you pretend to be? And for months?"

Mrs. Ardingley sighed. "Perhaps you should close the door."

"I don't owe you any favors. No one is in the corridor."

Mrs. Ardingley shrank back. "Perhaps I like using a wheelchair."

"That's nonsense."

"Look," Mrs. Ardingley said quickly. "I really did injure my legs. But then my health improved. We still needed money. And I hoped the duke might be compelled to feel sorry for Mr. Ardingley if I was, well, in a chair. If I went about walking, he would think that there was no reason in the world to give us any funds."

"Mr. Ardingley is his son though."

She shrugged. "Mr. Ardingley has worked so much more than his younger brother. And he is so much more appropriate as a duke."

"So you wanted to manipulate an elderly man's emotion?"

"For Rhys? Yes."

"You love him."

Mrs. Ardingley flushed. "Nonsense. You're a romantic."

"Don't be embarrassed," Cora said. "You did marry him."

"I did." Mrs. Ardingley gave her an assessing gaze. "Be careful with that...photographer."

"He's a PI."

"I hardly see the difference. None of us do. He hides in bushes and takes pictures. He's just one lacking in artistry."

Cora blew the air from her mouth.

"I saw the way your eyes lit up when you saw him this morning. It blinds you. To other things. I speak from experience."

Cora stiffened. "I didn't know you were watching us. Besides, there's nothing between Mr. Hall and me."

"Oh, darling, I wouldn't fault you." Mrs. Ardingley smiled, and in that moment, she could have been any society woman.

What would Mrs. Ardingley's life have been like if she hadn't felt that the only thing she had to offer her husband was her money? Would she have murdered her father-in-law in the optimistic hope that he might have set aside sufficient money to keep her husband in tailored clothing and with a healthy wine stock? Was that why she was waiting to reveal the fact that she'd recovered strength in her legs?

"Does Mr. Ardingley inherit any money from his father's will?"

"I don't know," Mrs. Ardingley said, but her eyes flickered to the side.

She's lying.

"Does your husband know?"

Mrs. Ardingley flushed and flicked her lashes down.

"You should tell him. There are enough secrets in this house." Cora left Mrs. Ardingley's room, thankful to see Randolph standing outside the duke's door.

Chapter Nineteen

Randolph opened the door to the duke's bedroom, and Cora entered behind him, conscious of his presence.

They stepped closer to the bed. The duke's body still lay there, still pinned by the chandelier.

Cora glanced at the ceiling, just in case there were more chandeliers that could come crashing down, but it was only the one. "I'm never going to put light fixtures over my bed."

"Is the room the same as when you last saw it?" Randolph asked.

"I think so," Cora said. "I mean, we were rather focused on the bed."

"And I can see why."

Cora stared at the corpse.

She despised this whole business of murder.

The duke's sensible woolen pajamas were stained with blood.

Randolph peered at the body. "We can see that blood, now dry, spurted from various punctures in the body. The chandelier hit his face and neck and chest. The good thing is we know when the murder happened. The room is so cold, I'm not sure we would have learned if he hadn't screamed. The pathologist would have struggled anyway."

"The murderer would have had to exit from the duchess's room."

"Why?"

"The door was locked."

He frowned. "That's odd."

"Why? He'd gone to bed."

"Locked doors are a hindrance to good service. We'll need to see if he made a habit of locking his door. Or if he was scared of anyone."

"He didn't seem to be the type to be scared of anything," Cora murmured.

Randolph tilted his head. "What were your impressions of him?"

"Not particularly good," Cora admitted. "He was set in his ways, certainly. He yelled at Veronica for tracking snow into the house. He wasn't afraid to humiliate people in front of others. He was eager to let them know where they ranked in importance to him, and that he was the most important person here. Always."

"Hmm." Randolph sighed. "Men like that could have made many enemies."

"Even far into the past."

"Perhaps. Who came to the door first?"

"Signor Palombi—or whatever his true name is. Lady Audrey and the dowager duchess came soon after, and Mrs. Ardingley was the last person to arrive."

"And the servants?"

"Wexley, the butler, arrived after someone rang. He and the other servants were taking their dinner in the kitchen."

"And where was the new duchess?"

"Veronica?" Cora blinked. "She was also approaching from the corridor when Edmund, Mr. Ardingley and I came up the steps."

"But you don't think she did it," Randolph said.

"No. Of course not."

Randolph returned his gaze to the chandelier. "There are some quite sharp pieces of crystal." He picked a piece up with his gloves carefully. "Look." He held it against one of the wounds. "See it fits perfectly. He must have a particular misfortune to have the crystal fall on his neck. It's managed to slice through his arteries."

Cora shivered. She wondered what other accidents could happen in this very old house.

"The marks are also quite deep," Randolph mused. "I wouldn't have thought a chandelier would produce it."

"You think something else killed him?"

"It's possible. Perhaps the murderer stabbed him with another weapon and tried to make it appear like an accident." He shrugged. "The murderer would have had to act quickly.

"Yes."

The base of the chandelier lay on the body. Randolph put on gloves and examined the chandelier's cord. "Ah, ha. This looks tampered with. You were right. Let me check the screws." He murmured to himself, and Cora was quiet, conscious that the man was focusing on all manner of complex things. Then Randolph drew back. "The screws are all tight. Someone wanted it to appear that the weight of the chandelier made it fall. If the murderer undid the screws he or she would have had to screw them back in again to make it appear like an accident."

"Then you do think it was murder?"

"I doubt there was somebody in the attic accidentally cutting cords." He glanced up at the ceiling. "But this process was done neatly. It was organized."

"We're looking for an organized murderer?"

He smiled. "How would you rate the organizational skills of the people here?"

"I don't think they've ever needed to display any skills, what with the servants."

"Perhaps the question is then...is there anyone who could not have been capable of undoing the chandelier and placing it on the body? Perhaps the dowager duchess?"

Cora shook her head. "I think she could have done it."

"I would like to question the suspects," Randolph said.

Cora almost bristled. "That word is so harsh."

"Less harsh than murderer."

"Yes. I spoke with some other guests this morning. I still haven't spoken with Lady Audrey or for that matter that much with Veronica."

"Then let's speak with them first," Randolph said.

"In the drawing room?"

"Why don't we speak with them in the location the duke was perhaps most at home in? The library."

Chapter Twenty

The library was filled with thick jewel-colored leather tomes. A large globe perched on a table, and busts dotted the room. The windows were stained glass, as if the designer had confused the solemnity of books with the solemnity of the church.

The walls were painted a deep garnet, and the ceilings were paneled. It looked warm and almost cozy, and utterly different from anything Cora had seen in Hollywood before.

Veronica glided into the room, all elegance. "Cora, darling. The butler said you wanted to see me in here. Whatever for?"

"We had some questions about the murder. Randolph Hall will be assisting."

"Oh."

Cora waited for outrage to spurt from Veronica's mouth, but she only smiled prettily.

"You must be the photographer who trespassed onto my property," Veronica said.

"Private investigator."

"Not an improvement, darling." She shrugged. "Well, Cora, if you find it important, I suppose we could chat. Heavens knows there's nothing else to do here."

"Could you tell me about the events of yesterday?" Randolph asked. "It's nice to make sure everyone's facts match."

"Oh, I do hope mine match!" she exclaimed. "This is really not something I'm used to. One doesn't expect to have to remember everything. Would you like some whisky? My husband thinks I don't know why his father liked going to the library." She strolled to fetch the alcohol.

"It's not necessary," Randolph said.

"Oh, but it's my pleasure!" She poured three fingers.

Randolph did not take a sip. Instead, he moved to the next question.

"What time did you arrive here?"

"Early afternoon. We'd missed lunch, but they sent us some cold food to our rooms." She wrinkled her nose. "Not that I am a big eater. I have other vices." Veronica grasped hold of the crystal tumbler and brought it elegantly to her mouth. "Scottish. So divine. So delicious. So decadent."

"What did you do after you arrived?"

"I took a nap." She looked at Cora. "I'm sorry I was such bad company."

"Oh, no," Cora said quickly. "I did the same."

Veronica smiled.

"And then what happened?" Randolph asked.

"I woke up."

"Anything unusual about the evening?"

"Well, it was dreadfully dull," Veronica said. "At least until the scream sounded, and then it was just dreadful."

She blinked. She'd stopped smiling, and her eyes widened as if still seeing the horror.

"Why didn't you join your husband and friend in the drawing room after dinner?"

Her eyes narrowed, and Cora remembered that Veronica was now a duchess. "Oh, I intended to. I went to change my clothes."

"For hours?"

"I was waiting for my maid," Veronica said. "I really didn't want to wear my silk gown when velvet was there, newly hung up. Far too chilly. It would have been quite wasted on Edmund and Cora. My maid never appeared though—apparently I'd been forgotten."

"So you heard the scream," Randolph continued. "What did it sound like?"

"Oh, it was dreadful. Ghastly. I rushed from my room into the corridor."

"Who was first in the room?"

"I'm not sure. It was locked. We were trying to get in. We were banging on the door and shouting. I hope those weren't the last things he heard." She gave a brave smile. "And then it was dark, though the balcony door was open which provided sufficient moonlight for us to know that something very wrong had occurred."

"Describe the scene."

"It was really too dreadful. The chandelier was splayed over the bed. Crystal shards everywhere. Some still sticking into his skin. And his eyes—they were wide open. But he," she gave a slight sob, "He was dead. He might have been a man with a very large voice and a dismissive manner, but he—really, he was quite frail when it came down to it. So thin. Quite...quite pathetic, actually. The chandelier was just sitting on him, crushing him. There was so much blood."

"It's odd that the crystal could do that."

She shrugged. "I'm an actress, honey. Not a physicist. The chandelier bars helped. Bad luck that he didn't move. I suppose you can't help how chandeliers are going to fall, and it's just so terribly unfortunate that the shattered crystals pierced him in a, well, fatal manner."

"It's possible the chandelier may have been tampered with."

"It is sweet that you're concerned, but my husband assures me the inquest will declare it entirely accidental."

Randolph leaned back. "We did expect you to say that."

"It wouldn't be right if I sat here across from you and divulged suspicions that my husband, mother-in-law, or one of their guests committed the murder."

"I understand." Randolph gave Veronica a curt, businesslike nod. His expression remained neutral: despite his occasional boyish behavior, these conversations suited him.

"I shall never forget the sight as long as I live," Veronica said. "It was so dreadful."

"And then you all went straight to bed?"

"Yes."

"Did your husband join you?"

"Naturally."

"If it was murder, who do you think did it?" Cora asked.

"I don't believe anyone here did it," Veronica said. "He was a nasty man. One would rather imagine he'd had enemies of his own from his business dealings."

"What did he think of you?"

"I believe you are more aware of his disdain for me than anyone. After all, he hired you to search for sordid secrets from my past."

Randolph flushed.

"The duke didn't approve of my fame. He likely would have preferred for his son to marry someone more prim and proper."

"Is Lady Audrey prim and proper?" Randolph asked.

Veronica straightened. "What makes you ask?"

"She's the only unattached woman here."

"Besides Cora."

"The late duke had not had the pleasure of meeting Cora before this gathering."

"Lady Audrey is really quite dull," Veronica said. "One does tend to have higher expectations of outrageousness for artists. I suppose it might be difficult for them to live up to them."

"I take it you do not find her to have bohemian tendencies."

"The woman wears tweed. Need I say more?"

Randolph was silent, and Veronica downed her whisky in a quick, elegant move. "Personally, I think Lady Audrey uses her portrait painting as an excuse to gain entry to all these great houses. Modern art has made it possible for anyone to declare themselves an artist, no matter how little training they've had or if they are even able to paint a straight line."

"I see."

Veronica shrugged. "On the other hand... I'm sure some women find it unnerving to have an artist do one's portrait when one is well aware that that artist is in the habit of having prostitutes splay before him for months without as much as a fig leaf to cover them."

"Tell me about the dowager duchess."

"I presume you would like me to cut to the chase and tell you if I think her capable of murder? Because I really can't sit around and accuse my mother-in-law of such heinous acts. They didn't seem particularly happy, but I can't imagine her sneaking into his room to murder him."

Cora recalled the duchess's damp slippers. "She had the most opportunity of anyone."

Veronica shrugged. "She was wealthy before the murder, and she will remain wealthy after. I'm not sure that being bored with one's aging husband is enough to compel one to murder him, no matter how conveniently chandeliers are placed."

"She is also not English."

"As someone who is not English," Veronica said, "I resist the implication that not being English would make her more murderous."

"Did she talk often of Czechoslovakia?"

"No."

"Tell me about Mr. Ardingley."

"He's charming." She frowned. "Though he has a surprising temper."

"And his wife?"

"Is less charming, though I believe she possesses the same temper. Of course, Mrs. Ardingley is less capable of demonstrating the sort of physical prowess that could lead to murder."

"Did they strike you as a good couple?"

"Not in particular, though I've wondered if they are fonder of each other than they let on. They're certainly never indifferent."

"Do you believe either of them would have had a motive for murder?" Randolph asked, not dwelling on Mrs. Ardingley's ambulatory abilities.

Veronica glanced at the filing cabinet. "It depends what was in his will. Rhys wanted to be recognized—I'm not sure he was. I don't think he knew."

"You've been very helpful," Randolph said and strode to the filing cabinet.

"Oh, good," Veronica said. "If you want to reward me, you can always destroy any evidence you have of my improper upbringing. For some reason, people seem to find rags-to-riches stories far more compelling for men, even though it's harder for us women to make our way."

Veronica tossed her hair and exited the library. Cora and Randolph were alone.

"What are you doing?" a voice asked.

Edmund stood in the entrance to the library with Lady Audrey behind him.

Chapter Twenty-one

Suspicion seemed to flicker over both Edmund's and Lady Audrey's faces.

"The butler said we could use this room to conduct interviews," Randolph said.

"I suppose it would make it safer for those of us who are not vicious murderers," Lady Audrey remarked.

"If you think so," Edmund acquiesced, and his gaze moved to the filing cabinet. "Still, I'm not comfortable with a stranger sorting through father's things."

"Very well." Randolph flashed Edmund a broad grin, but Cora suspected Randolph would find an occasion to search through the filing cabinet at a time when he did not have one of Britain's highest ranked aristocrats looking disapprovingly at him.

Lady Audrey shrugged. "What could he find? Besides, in a sense, he was your father's employee."

"Right." Edmund raked a hand through his hair. "Yes. I suppose so." He frowned. "Did my father pay you yet? I wouldn't want his death to have caused you any inconvenience."

"I was—er—paid in advance. It would be nice to speak with you about the event of last night," Randolph said.

"I already mentioned some details to Miss Clarke," Edmund said quickly.

Randolph nodded. "Perhaps Lady Audrey..."

"Oh. You want to question me?"

"Please," Randolph said.

Lady Audrey settled opposite Randolph and Cora. She seemed a trifle uneasy and darted a glance toward Edmund.

"I don't mean to make you uncomfortable," Randolph assured her.

"I'm not." Lady Audrey assessed Randolph. "You just look somewhat familiar. Have we met before?"

He paused, but then grinned. "Only if you have a habit of getting in trouble with the law."

Lady Audrey's cheeks turned a ruddy color, her embarrassment evidently not hampered by her abundance of freckles. "I must have been mistaken."

Edmund frowned. "I would hardly conflate being a private detective with the law."

"Then perhaps you have more to learn about the law," Randolph said easily.

"Hmph. I'll leave you be." Edmund exited the room.

"What brings you to Chalcroft Park?" Randolph asked.

"I grew up next door. In Oak Manor," Lady Audrey said.

"Mm...hmm. And how did you come to be invited?"

Lady Audrey flushed. "I suppose you could say I was angling for an invite. An utter mistake, given the circumstances."

"So they invited you out of pity?" Randolph asked.

"Naturally not," Lady Audrey said. "I offered to do a portrait of the Duchess of Hawley and the new—er—Lady Holt."

"I see. And what did the late duke think about this?"

"We got on well enough. He could be abrasive at times. He respected my family, though."

"It must have been difficult growing up near a man so prone to criticizing people."

Lady Audrey raised an eyebrow. "Rudeness is not a trait unique to him." She smiled. "Murder would ruin my reputation; being a freeloader is sufficiently intolerable."

"Are you in dire economic straights?"

"Nonsense. Most people are lining up at soup kitchens. Not me. But I've limited myself to only one maid and cook in my London townhouse. Quite disgraceful, I know." She glanced at Cora. "I suppose you, of all people, can understand the convenience of accepting invitations to house parties."

Cora flushed. "And you weren't close to your parents?"

"They always go to the French Riviera in winter. It would be nice to pop round to their house sometime, if this infernal snow is ever clears. It's within walking distance."

"So take us through the events of the night. What time did you arrive here?"

"Oh, I've been here for several days already. It's Thursday now? I arrived on Monday. They're really not all that dreadful. I was painting the Duchess of Hawley."

"Did she like your portrait?"

"Oh, I think she was amused enough by it. She didn't like standing still much, and the duke naturally was not enthralled by the style, but on the whole, I suppose it was a positive experience."

"So you were alone here with Lord Holt."

She shrugged. "Yes, Edmund and I were able to catch up."

Something about her manner made Cora think about Veronica's reaction to him. "Have you ever been romantically entwined with him?"

"Edmund?" She laughed and then stopped. "Ages ago and utterly silly. We get along quite well. Always have."

"It would have been convenient to marry someone like Lord Holt. Did you ever expect a proposal?"

Lady Audrey smiled. "You sound like my aged grandmother. Edmund is...like a brother."

"Where were you when the duke died?" Cora asked.

"In bed."

"Did you hear anything in the corridor?"

She shook her head. "I wish I had. If he was really murdered—" She sighed. "I wish I could have prevented it somehow."

"Is there anything you remember that might be useful?"

She frowned. "I heard footsteps outside my door at, hmm, perhaps ten o'clock."

Signor Palombi.

"Who do you think may have killed the duke?"

"Mr. and Mrs. Ardingley despised him. They thought the duke should provide greater support to Mr. Ardingley."

"And what were your opinions on that?"

"I thought His Grace was already being remarkably generous. Most men don't invite their byblows for the holidays. Most don't even acknowledge their bastards, but everyone in society knows that Rhys is the duke's firstborn and illegitimate son." She shrugged. "He should consider himself fortunate."

"Any other impressions? Was the duke stressed with anything? Perhaps business?"

"Not business," Lady Audrey said. "He liked to boast about how many people from different countries were approaching him. I do know he was deeply uncomfortable with Edmund's new wife. I think Edmund's parents always assumed that Edmund and I would marry. Veronica, of course, is nothing like me, and her past threatens the family's reputation. The duke was plotting how he might sever Edmund's relationship with Veronica."

"Even though it's a new dukedom?"

"Especially because of that," Lady Audrey said.

"You can go," Randolph said to Lady Audrey. "You've been helpful."

Lady Audrey nodded. She turned at the door. "Good luck. I hope you find the culprit."

"Thank you." Cora smiled.

Randolph rose immediately. "Let's look through the filing cabinet."

"I don't think I can go through his private things," Cora said.

"Then I'll search it," Randolph said.

"Fine."

"You can fetch someone else for us to interview."

"We should speak with the butler," Cora said.

"You think he had a motive?" Randolph asked.

"It's unlikely. He does have a good position. Why would he want to ruin that? All the same, perhaps he noticed something."

"Fine. Ring the bell for him." He grinned. "You can keep watch outside."

Chapter Twenty-two

Cora exited the library.

"Miss Clarke," somebody whispered.

Cora turned around.

There didn't seem to be anybody.

At least...not at first.

But then she spotted the tips of a pair of distinctly plain shoes behind one of the oversized blue and white vases that seemed to adorn the manor house as if it had been at one time intended as a museum of the Orient.

A head peeked out. Blonde locks fell under a starched cap.

"Gladys?"

Scarlet painted lips swept into a wide smile. "You're here."

"Why yes."

"I had hoped you would be," Gladys said. "I'm not exactly supposed to be in this section of the house."

"Oh?"

"I'm not a footman," Gladys said, frowning. "And it's not morning, and the fires don't need to be lit."

"I won't tell anyone I saw you."

Gladys smiled. "Oh, I knew you wouldn't, miss. You're not like the others."

"Th-thank you," Cora stammered.

"I'm not playing hooky, miss," Gladys said. "I think that's the term you use in all those American films."

"Probably not the best weather for it," Cora said.

Gladys snorted. "Indeed not."

"Did you want to tell me something in particular?" Cora asked.

Gladys's cheeks turned rosy. "I'm probably being silly. It's likely nothing, miss. And lord knows it's not nice to gossip."

Cora waited for Gladys to continue. The maid seemed occupied with flicking her gaze this way or that, as if hoping to gain confidence from the furnishings.

"But it might be important," Gladys said. "I mean, if there hadn't been a murder, I wouldn't say anything, but..."

"You can tell me," Cora said.

Gladys drew in a deep breath. "I never wanted to betray anyone's trust. I'm a servant. I'm beholden to the family. And I do hate gossip."

Gladys's eyes sparkled, and Cora almost smiled. She suspected that Gladys's opinion of gossip was not entirely one of disdain.

"Miss Brown!" A deep baritone voice barreled toward them. "What are you doing here? Do you not know what time it is?"

The butler assessed Gladys. "You've got face paint on."

"Make up," Gladys said. "This isn't the nineteenth century. Or some carnival." Her lips twitched, and the butler's glower strengthened.

"Young lady," the butler said. "You'll get yourself in trouble one day."

Gladys lowered her head and left.

"You rang for me, Miss Clarke?" Wexley said.

"Mr. Randolph Hall did," she said. "I'll—er—just tell him you're here. Perhaps you might—er—bring some tea for us first."

"Very well, Miss Clarke." The butler left.

Cora entered the library. "Wexley will soon be here with tea."

"Splendid." Randolph shoved some papers inside a folder on the desk.

"I spoke with one of the maids too," Cora said, hating that her voice seemed to go up too high, as if it were scaling the keys on the right side of the piano. "Gladys. She was here. And then the butler scolded her for being in this room. Isn't that odd?"

Randolph nodded slowly, but his face had a thoughtful expression.

Perhaps the rule might not be considered particularly eccentric to English people.

"She wanted to tell me something," Cora said. "But she left before she could."

"I imagine it was about one of your dresses," Randolph said. "Perhaps she wasn't certain about the ironing technique for US clothes."

Cora frowned. "Surely it wouldn't vary."

"You drive on the wrong side of the road in America," Randolph said. "Who knows in what strange manner your dressmakers might fashion your garments?"

Cora blinked. "Perhaps one of my clothes had a missing button."

"Right," Randolph said. "Perhaps that was—er—more likely."

Wexley arrived soon after, and Randolph beamed. "Take a seat."

"Very well, Mr. Hall."

"Good. Tell me, have you gotten any word from the outside world?"

"No," Wexley sighed.

"Have all the servants been accounted for?"

"They're all here. Except for young Billy of course. He volunteered to inform the police, since the telephone lines are still not working. I hope they can arrive tomorrow."

"How do you find working here?" Randolph asked.

"This is certainly far better than most." He smiled with the confidence of a man who'd worked all his life to get a good position and had achieved it.

"How long have you been with this family?"

"Some twenty years. I've known the new master since he was a boy. Before that I was a footman, though thankfully no one can remember that now." He gazed into the middle distance, perhaps recollecting his well-positioned tables and prompt refilling at wine at dinner parties that at long last had earned him his promotion.

"What are your impressions of your employers?"

"It's not my place to reflect on that," Wexley said.

"Someone here may have murdered someone else," Randolph reminded him. "We just want to protect people."

"Anything you can say can be ever so helpful," Cora said. "Even small things."

"I don't see how."

"We'll compare it to what other people said. We might discover patterns, confirmations or strange contradictions that can lead us to the murderer."

"I suppose these are unconventional times," Wexley said.

"Can you please detail the events of this week?" Randolph asked. "Was there anything out of the ordinary? Anything that had upset the duke?"

"The duke was given to being upset. He was passionate. Far better suited to be leading an army into battle. He might have made a good factory foreman as well, though we wouldn't like to tell him that."

"Was there anything he was particularly concerned about this week?"

"I wouldn't be able to tell you anything. The master might be dead, but he wouldn't want me to divulge his secrets." He tilted his head. "He was going to meet with his solicitor after Christmas."

"To change his will?"

"I think he was interested in making queries as to how he could limit his son's access to his estate after his death. He was doing the same for his wife." The butler's lips twitched. "He was even considering donating to charity as a means of diminishing the extent of Lord Holt's inheritance. One wonders how many charities have received money because of people's discomfort with their relatives."

"The house, though, would still have passed to the duke?"

"Yes. He is the heir."

"Do you have an opinion on who may have harmed the duke?"

"Not at all. I was, as you know, in the servants' quarters. I am afraid I can shed no light."

"Hmph. Thank you all the same."

Chapter Twenty-three

Cora half wondered if Gladys would appear in her room to dress her for dinner. But she did not. Likely she had remembered that Cora was wearing her one black dress already and had deemed it not necessary to make an appearance. Cora was quite capable of putting on her jewelry by herself and she redid her makeup.

She made her way downstairs. Perhaps one of the people in this manor house was a murderer, but she still possessed little desire to be by herself in her room.

Darkness had fallen over the house once again, despite the servants' valiant attempts to light fires and candles. Long shadows loomed over every room, and even objects like vases seemed imbued with sinister qualities.

"Hello, Cora." Randolph gave her his normal big smile when she entered the library. Her heart managed to flutter, and she frowned.

She should be used to his presence by now.

She raised her chin. What was so special about broad shoulders and chiseled facial features after all?

Heavens knew that Hollywood had been filled with men of above average appearance.

But somehow, Randolph was different.

But Randolph didn't see her as a child actress, given to obediently reciting lines and learning complex choreography.

He'd somehow managed to procure an evening suit, and he looked suave and cultured and utterly unlike the photographer figure she'd once imagined him to be.

"The others are in the dining room," he said.

"You met them?"

"All of them."

"And they were..."

"Frosty. Fortunately, the blustery north wind rather prepares one for cold behavior, whether the temperature or the temperament sort."

"How fortuitous. And have you discovered the murderer?"

"No. Though tonight promises to be fun. Mr. Ardingley managed to convince Lady Denisa to hold a buffet."

"How terribly modern."

"His wife was apparently hiding the fact, even from him, that she'd regained strength in her legs, and he wants to use the occasion to celebrate her improved health."

Cora smiled.

Randolph scrutinized her. "You knew already."

"Not for long though."

"Hmph."

"Miss Clarke!" Mr. Ardingley's voice was gleeful. "Come in here. It's a party."

"Oh, Rhys," the dowager hushed. "That might not be the correct word to use. Last night at this time my husband was busy dying."

"Today is a new day, and tomorrow a newer, better one still," Mr. Ardingley said. "My wife, it seems, has experienced a miracle. She can walk."

"How wonderful," Cora said.

She didn't mention that Mrs. Ardingley was the same woman she'd always been and walking should not influence the man's opinion of her.

"It's jolly good news. She hid it for my sake," Mr. Ardingley said. "She was worried the improvement of her health might incline my so swiftly departed father to not reserve any money for me in his will."

"Indeed."

"Indeed." Mr. Ardingley beamed as if his wife had filled the Queen Mary high with red roses for him.

"Ah, Cora!" Veronica waved at her from across the room. She wore a striking magenta gown and a sheer ebony scarf.

Cora blinked.

"You needn't look so shocked, dear. You know quite well that I had no black evening gown. The scarf is black at least."

"It's mostly see-through."

"So it is," Veronica frowned. "Next time I will know that even if I'm not visiting anyone in the least bit ill, there is apparently a possibility that someone will be murdered during a snowstorm when all the shops are inaccessible."

"I'm sorry. I only thought it appeared a trifle flamboyant."

"Stylish, honey."

"Yes."

"Besides," Veronica said, "my bracelet is ebony. I'm sure it must count."

A broche pince of pink tourmaline and rock crystal shaped in a pyramid sat on the admittedly black band.

"It doesn't look particularly sober," Cora said.

"It's French, honey." Veronica linked arms with Cora and led her to a long table where the others were selecting cold meats and breads to put on their plates. "Do have some food. We might do some dancing after dinner."

"We're going to dance now," Mr. Ardingley roared. "Somebody, play some piano."

Randolph settled down on the piano seat.

"Did you know he could play?" Veronica asked.

Cora shook her head.

Possibly this could go quite poorly.

In the next moment Randolph placed his hands on the keys. He winked at Cora, and she stepped back.

And then Randolph played.

He'd chosen an upbeat melody, not caring that the length of time between the notes was minute, nor that his fingers had to practically dash across the keys.

"Well, I'm impressed." Veronica turned to Cora. "Sorry, darling. I really must find Edmund. This calls for a dance."

Mr. Ardingley seemed to have come to a similar conclusion for he swept Mrs. Ardingley into his arms, and she clung to him as he moved her across the makeshift dance floor.

"We should have had this event in the ballroom," the dowager murmured. "My dear husband would be horrified to see them now."

Cora glanced at the dowager duchess.

She should be the most distraught of all of them. The dowager duchess seemed to have gotten over her horror at her husband's death and was already well on her way to enjoying an active widowhood. She glided about the room, ensuring that the servants were providing the best canapés and refilling their guests' glasses.

Had she murdered her husband? Was she celebrating?

An uneasy feeling moved through Cora. It seemed wrong to partake in pleasures at such a point, and yet... who was she to question them? Once the police arrived and finished their inquiries, they would likely disperse.

"More champagne?" The butler lowered a silver platter filled with gold rimmed champagne flutes.

Cora inhaled the bubbly aroma, but she shook her head.

"Very well," the butler said, moving to Veronica.

The music turned to a new song, but Mrs. Ardingley and Mr. Ardingley remained on the dance floor.

Footsteps sounded behind her, and she turned.

Edmund stood before her. "It is ghastly how they're all enjoying Father's death, isn't it?"

"I wouldn't say they're enjoying it," Cora said loyally.

"Don't," Edmund said. "My eyes are fully functioning. I wasn't aware that my sister-in-law's lips were *able* to spread into such an upward direction."

Cora giggled. "Perhaps they do seem a trifle relaxed."

"That's better," Edmund said. "Now, tell me, which of them do you think did it?"

Cora jerked her head. "The inquest will determine if it was a murder."

Edmund shrugged. "You and that strange photographer man interviewed my childhood friend."

Cora's cheeks flushed.

"And I have relative faith in the ability of the servants to maintain the house well enough that the occupants are not accidently crushed by crystal objects," Edmund continued.

"I'm sorry again for your loss," Cora said.

"Don't be. Even father would have been quite tickled about the uniqueness of his murder."

"He didn't seem happy about it when it happened," Cora said, recalling the terrified scream.

"No," Edmund said thoughtfully, "he didn't."

Cora nibbled on the bread and cheese.

"It feels sacrilegious to eat this in here," Edmund said. "Father demanded five different courses at dinner."

Cora ate the rest of her food and approached Randolph at the piano. "You play quite well."

"Apparently you do the same." He grinned. "Take a seat."

Cora squeezed in beside him, conscious that only inches separated them on the piano stool.

She moved her hands over the keys.

Music came easily to her.

It was comforting to know the order to place her fingers.

It was all written in black and white sheet notes before her.

The modicum of emotion she could add was just that—a modicum.

And in the meantime, she could let herself be carried away by the sweet melody.

"Honey!" Veronica approached them. "You shouldn't be working."

"It's hardly work."

Veronica rolled her eyes. "You would think so. Not playing music was one of the chief benefits of getting older parts. I haven't played anything since my last *Backyard Bonanza* film. You should perhaps fetch the gramophone. Otherwise you'll be tied to the piano all night."

"I don't mind."

Veronica grinned and lowered her voice. "But that handsome detective might."

Cora flushed.

"I sent Gladys ages ago to get the gramophone, and she still hasn't appeared. Would you please fetch it? Your heels are so much less tall than mine. I wouldn't call them shoes at all."

"Very well," Cora said.

"You don't have to do everything she desires," Randolph said.

"I wouldn't," Cora said. "But this gives me the chance to find Gladys. She did want to tell me something important."

"Yes." Randolph's face was inscrutable. "It's good you remembered that."

"Is everything all right?"

"It will be."

Cora nodded and hurried up the stairs. "Gladys? Gladys?"

No servant came.

Well, it was late.

She'd wished the butler hadn't chased the maid away. He had certainly had no interesting information to share with Randolph and herself.

Perhaps she should go downstairs.

She went to get the gramophone, and as she browsed through Veronica's collection of records, a smile formed on her lips. Veronica only had big band music. No classical at all. She chose some records and left the room. The gramophone was somewhat unwieldy, and she wished that she hadn't grabbed so many records.

Still, she made her way down the stairs. At least Randolph would no longer be constrained to playing the piano.

The man did play remarkably well. She stepped off the staircase and onto one of the sumptuous Oriental carpets when—

The rug seemed to be pulled from beneath her.

Cora pitched forward.

The gramophone and records clattered to the floor.

Cora blinked.

The chandelier certainly was not supposed to be in her eyesight.

Someone had *made* her fall.

The chandelier arms seemed to gleam menacingly at her, and with a start, she rolled off the carpet.

The chandelier did not plummet to the floor.

Naturally not.

Why would it?

"Cora?" Randolph called out.

"Randolph!"

He rushed toward her. "I heard the commotion."

"I fell."

"I see that." His lips didn't twitch, and his expression exuded concern. Randolph offered her his hand and pulled her up easily.

"You were supposed to be playing piano," Cora said.

"I didn't like to see you wandering this big house by yourself. It can be dangerous."

Cora nodded. Her breath seemed caught in her throat, and something must have shown on her face, for he swept her into his arms.

"My poor darling."

"What was that racket?" Mr. and Mrs. Ardingley came through the corridor, followed soon by the others.

"I fell," Cora said.

It seemed silly to say someone pulled up the carpet.

She hadn't seen anyone, and the first person who'd appeared had been Randolph.

"The gramophone looks ruined," Veronica said in dismay.

"I'm sorry," Cora murmured.

"Perhaps it wasn't the most appropriate occasion after all," Veronica conceded.

Cora gave her a wobbly smile.

Chapter Twenty-four

A door slammed, and Cora jerked her eyes open.

"Forgive me, miss," a woman said. "I did not mean to wake you."

Cora turned toward the voice.

It didn't sound like Gladys.

"It's just that I'm carrying all this tea," the woman said apologetically. "Mind if I draw the curtains?"

"Go ahead," Cora said, her voice groggy. Tea sounded absolutely delightful.

Shuffling sounded, and Cora realized that some papers were being moved to the side and a tray set on the table near the door. The woman drew the drapes, and light spilled into the room.

The air remained far too frigid, and the rubber water bottle at the foot of her bed felt uncomfortable. She pulled herself farther up and tightened the blanket about her. It seemed an inadequate barrier against the cold.

"I'll come back and light the fire," the new maid said. "But we thought you would like your tea now." She hesitated. "Do you need any help dressing?"

"I can manage," Cora said.

Relief inundated the woman's face. "Oh, good. I ain't never dressed anyone before. I would try not to pull the buttons off, but..."

"It's fine," Cora said. "I'm happy to manage on my own. Where is Gladys?"

"Oh, you miss 'er already," the maid said, her voice mournful. "I knew you would."

"No," Cora said quickly. "I-I was just curious."

She hated the distraught sound in the woman's voice.

"What's your name?" Cora asked.

"It's Becky, miss. And Miss Clarke—we 'aven't seen 'er. I'm not supposed to be 'ere. Golly, it is awfully grand." She tilted her head toward the paneled ceiling.

"Yes," Cora agreed.

"I wouldn't be 'ere," the servant continued. "But the 'ouse is full. Cook is busy with breakfast, and Gladys is gone."

"She left? In this snow?" Cora glanced through the window.

The snow still fell, and large untouched snow drifts formed into a series of hills that Cora was sure had not existed when she arrived. The sky was a forbidding gray, and Cora's stomach tightened.

Gladys had wanted to speak with her yesterday. Had it been important?

Had she known who the murderer was? Had she left to avoid him?

Or her?

Cora frowned.

That couldn't be it.

After all, Gladys would have found a way to tell her or one of the head servants, if she'd known the murderer's identity. It had sounded as if Gladys had had some sort of gossip. Had it been more serious than Gladys realized?

"We need to find her," Cora said, rising from the bed.

The new maid's eyes filled with tears. "I am that bad, am I?"

She handed Cora a teacup and saucer.

Milky tea spilled onto the saucer, and when she took a sip, the liquid was cold. Cora refrained from remarking on either imperfect state.

"Nonsense," Cora assured her. "I'm just worried about her."

"Nah," the maid said. "Don't worry. Gladys is always fine. She's awfully clever. Even uses a typewriter."

"Does she?"

The servant beamed. "Right complicated it is too knowing where all 'em keys go."

"Are you very good friends with her?"

"She's my cousin," the maid said. "Got me this job too. Only a trial basis." She frowned. "I don't think the trial is going well. Cook says I'm lucky there are so many guests 'ere and that there's a blizzard and they can't get anyone else."

"I'm sure you'll feel right at home with the job soon," Cora said, and the maid beamed.

"I'll go light the fire," Becky said, nearing the Oriental screen that sat before it, guarding the room from any wayward sparks.

"Splendid." Cora took a sip of tea. Earl Grey was becoming her favorite, and she appreciated the subtle hints of London.

An anguished scream filled the air.

Becky!

With trembling hands, Cora quickly fumbled her teacup back in its saucer. She sprang from the bed and scurried toward the maid. "What happened?"

Becky turned to her, her face white and distraught. "I'm afraid I found Gladys, miss."

"How? Where?"

Becky pointed slowly to the fireplace.

A pair of legs stuck out. The legs could be termed shapely, and the ankles could certainly be termed thin. The shoes were glossy, patent leather, even though ash clung to them.

"I'll—er—get her down," Becky said, approaching the body.

"N-no. Perhaps the police—" She stopped as Becky jerked down the body.

It was Gladys.

Not Gladys as Cora knew her.

Not laughing.

Not touching up her makeup.

Not about to launch into some great gossip.

No, this Gladys was dead.

Cora's heart tightened.

It was the second time she'd seen a dead body.

Gladys lay on her back, her eyes wide with shock. Bruises ravaged her neck.

"It's 'er," the new maid wailed. She sank her head down. "Can you save 'er, miss?"

Cora shook her head. "No one can. See how stiff her body is? She must have been dead for hours. Perhaps all night."

"Oh, Lord." The servant sank to her knees. "Poor Gladys."

"Yes."

It was tragic.

Oh, so tragic.

Guilt surged through Cora.

Gladys had wanted to tell her something yesterday evening, but she'd allowed Wexley to chase her away. Gladys had termed it gossip, and Cora had acquiesced to Gladys's belief that it might not be important and was perhaps needlessly ridiculous.

Footsteps pattered in the corridor, no doubt alerted by Becky's scream, and soon everyone stood in Cora's room, assessing the maid's body.

Chapter Twenty-five

"Two murders in two days," the dowager duchess bemoaned. "That is outrageous."

Cora frowned. "You weren't sure the late duke's death was a murder—"

"I'm certain now," said the dowager duchess. "And please refer to him as your father. Not his occupation, no matter how much pride he found in it."

Everyone gathered around the body, and Cora wrapped her robe more tightly around her.

She'd been sad when the duke had died, but she hadn't particularly liked him, and he'd had decades of partaking in sumptuous pleasure behind him.

Gladys, though, had scarcely lived. She'd wanted to do so, to be sure. She'd been bright and curious. Gladys hadn't been involved in selling arms to a country that had fought a long and bloody battle with Britain a generation ago, and was rumored to be interested in having another go at a war, though this time with the intention of winning. Gladys didn't have children to whom she was cruel.

Gladys had had her whole life before her, and even if others might make snide comments about her inability to stay quiet and her enthusiasm for everything fashionable, Cora was certain that Gladys had never intended to harm anyone.

It seemed unimaginably cruel that someone had harmed Gladys in this manner.

"She wanted to see me yesterday," Cora said sadly. "And then she changed her mind and had to return to the kitchen. If only I had insisted she tell me what was troubling her."

"You think she was killed because she had information against someone?" Randolph asked.

Cora gave a miserable nod.

"What's that in the chimney?" Lady Audrey asked.

"I don't see—"

Lady Audrey bent down and pulled up a long piece of leather.

"That's hardly elegant," Veronica said. "Is that some horrid belt?"

"Gladys had excellent taste," Becky said defensively.

"I don't think Gladys would have used that as a belt." She picked up the fabric. It looked—familiar.

Too familiar.

She glanced at Randolph. "Do you have your camera?"

"It's in my room,"

"Why do you ask?" Edmund asked.

"I just think—it might be, I mean it looks awfully similar to—"

"A camera strap" Veronica finished for her. "Honey, you really needn't stammer so much. I'm quite sure you added all sorts of extra words that you didn't need."

"I think someone else should search Randolph's room," Lady Audrey said.

"You don't mean to think I would have done anything? That's nonsense."

Distress moved through Cora.

Randolph knew spies—even the foreign ones.

Perhaps someone had hired Randolph to murder the duke.

He had arrived in the middle of the night.

Perhaps it was just like the dowager duchess had said—he was the strange man who'd killed the duke and then had had second thoughts about attempting to leave the property because of the snow.

"Becky, please bring us Mr. Hall's camera," the dowager ordered.

"Very well, your grace." Becky curtsied and hurried from the room.

She came back quickly carrying a camera. Half of the strap was missing.

"She must have pulled it from his hand when he was killing her," Mr. Ardingley said.

"How dreadful!" Mrs. Ardingley buried her head on her husband's shoulder.

It is horrible.

Randolph had been perhaps an illusion.

Too perfect, too exquisite, too charming.

Cora's throat tightened, as if she'd managed to swallow some strychnine.

There was no way for anyone except a stranger to kill the duke.

They'd investigated, but found no one guilty.

There was a tree outside the window.

Naturally, Randolph would have said it was impossible for someone to have climbed it.

He'd been feeding her false information.

Gladys must have noticed something.

That's why she'd wanted to talk with Cora in private.

And Cora had been so foolish that she'd mentioned it to Randolph, sealing that poor maid's fate.

When she'd fallen, it had been Randolph who'd appeared.

Because he'd been right there.

Perhaps he hadn't wanted her to see where he'd come from, since he'd just slipped away to kill Gladys.

Randolph's eyes were thoughtful, and Cora despised them. He should be acting more afraid. She *knew.* The fact should make his body quiver, though Cora thought it possible he'd never had an unconfident moment in his life. The man oozed self-assurance...the sort only found in the murderers in the pictures.

"Maybe Randolph is the murderer," Cora said.

"Nonsense." Randolph gave a strangled laugh. "I wasn't even in the house when the murder took place."

"You climbed the tree. Or perhaps you even brought a ladder over from the barn. I don't know how you got inside, but you did."

"I didn't do it," he said solemnly. "I-I value life."

It would be so easy to believe him. He'd been her support over the past few days, but she shouldn't have been leaning against him. He was dangerous, as unstable as a drawstring bridge.

"You're coming with me," Edmund said.

"What are you doing?" Randolph's voice sounded almost desperate, but Edmund swept his arms behind him and tightened his grip.

"Don't run away," Edmund thundered.

Veronica looked like she was about to swoon. "You're so heroic, darling."

Edmund smiled. His face remained grave. "We won't have you murder anyone else here."

"But look," Randolph said desperately. "I didn't do it. You must believe me."

"You must have been hiding out," Cora said somberly. "And you had access to murder Gladys. And motive. Why else would she have your camera cord?"

"Evidently someone planted it there," he said.

"I agree," Signor Palombi said.

Cora glared at him. "You would. The police can decide when they arrive."

"Yes," Edmund said. "In the mean time we'll put you in the South Tower."

"This is when a dungeon would come in handy," Lady Denisa said. "It's a shame none of the former Holts ever took on the role of magistrate."

"You'll suffer for this." Edmund's voice was icy and cold. "Breaking into our house? Murdering my father? And then sitting in the drawing room and convincing Cora to arrange a bedroom for you? Interrogating all of us—pretending to help?"

"That poor sweet servant girl," the dowager wailed.

She'd probably never said so many nice things about a servant before.

"B-but," Randolph stammered. "Do something, Cora. Tell them!"

"I can't," Cora said sadly. She picked up the Shakespeare volume. "Take this with you. You can read it while you wait for the police."

Chapter Twenty-six

The snow had stopped, content with their transformation of the landscape. Pink and orange light sparkled over the slabs of snow. Some servants had ventured outside with shovels, and the sound of scraping and crunching snow passed through even the thick centuries-old glass windows.

"Let's get out of this dreary house," Veronica said. "It reeks of death and despair."

"What would you propose, darling?" Edmund asked.

"We could go ice skating," Veronica said. "We can't simply wait for the police to arrive."

"I think that's precisely what we should do," Cora said.

Edmund gave her a gentle smile. "We have the murderer already."

Cora's heart gave her a pang.

She'd liked Randolph...far too much.

But she'd clearly been utterly wrong about him.

"Look," Veronica said. "I'm sorry about him."

"He seemed so sweet," Cora said mournfully.

"It's still good we discovered him," she told Cora in a stern tone. "He was a murderer. Don't spend any time worrying about his fate. He doesn't deserve it. He didn't spend much time worrying about Gladys's fate."

"Maybe he wasn't really the murderer—"

"But there's still a strong chance he was, and if so, he should be locked up until the police arrive."

"You're right."

Veronica beamed. "Of course I am."

"Darling, you go and take anyone who wants to go ice skating with you," Edmund said. "I'll wait for the police to arrive."

"And I'll work on the dowager duchess's portrait," Lady Audrey said.

"Oh, yes, you stay," Veronica said. "Now. Who's going to go with me?"

Signor Palombi, the dowager, and Mr. and Mrs. Ardingley all expressed various degrees of enthusiasm.

"It's cold outside," Cora hedged. She didn't want to attempt to have a good time. Not now. Not when the first man she'd felt close to her in her whole life was locked in a tower. Not when he'd murdered two people.

"You'd probably prefer to lie in bed. But don't worry," Veronica said airily. "You can borrow a cashmere sweater from me. It is very cold out there."

Cora went to the room and opened Veronica's wardrobe. There were several cashmere options. Gladys had arranged everything neatly. Cora brushed her hand against the soft furs and silks and velvets, organized in a perfect display of colors starting at ivory and a silvery blue to the most vibrant crimson and emerald colors. There was no black.

Veronica was, despite everything, an optimist.

It was one of the many things Cora admired about her.

Clearly, she was wearing her only black clothes to honor her father-in-law's passing.

She grabbed a cashmere sweater and slid it over her shoulders. The material was so luxurious, and she twirled before the mirror.

She noticed the record box.

And frowned.

Where was *Horror Most Dreadful?* The main reason Veronica had brought the gramophone had been to listen to it. Why did she only have music records? Had she hidden it? And if so—why?

The police should arrive soon, she hoped. The roads were beginning to clear, and Veronica and her husband were already speaking about visiting Latin America for a holiday.

Cora frowned.

Veronica couldn't have used the record and gramophone to mimic the late duke's death.

Was it possible that...

Cora needed to listen to the record.

That scream *hadn't* sounded natural. But perhaps it could be heard on the record?

If the scream was on the record, then the murder could have happened earlier than they'd thought. The murderer could have killed the duke, perhaps by stabbing him and then removing the chandelier in the hopes of successfully making the murder appear like an accident.

Veronica could have murdered him.

Not some mysterious stranger.

She shook her head.

Veronica was Cora's friend.

She couldn't suspect her.

But how well did Cora really know her?

The duke had been trying to get dirt on Veronica. Perhaps he'd been blackmailing her. Perhaps she'd been pressed too far.

I need to find that record.

Cora searched the closet.

And then underneath the bed.

And finally, underneath the chest of drawers—and it was there.

She'd found it.

Cora tucked the record underneath her sweater and hurried downstairs.

"There you are," Veronica said.

"Yes," Cora squeaked.

She couldn't just accuse her friend of murder.

The police would arrive, and she could tell them of her suspicions... But they might laugh at her. It did seem ridiculous. And she didn't even know if such a scream appeared on the record.

If Cora could only be sure.

If only the gramophone were not broken. If only the roads were clear and she could purchase a gramophone in town.

Cora suddenly missed Los Angeles.

But perhaps...If she could find another one.

Lady Audrey.

Her home was nearby.

Perhaps her parents had one.

"I had such a dreadful experience skiing," Cora said. "I'm really not up for more new winter activities, I'm afraid."

"Oh, you poor dear," Veronica said. "It will be such fun."

Cora tried not to wince.

Two people had just been murdered.

No fun was supposed to take place now.

Cora had thought Veronica's flippancy somewhat of an act, but perhaps Cora had assumed what she'd desired to believe.

Perhaps she'd added hidden motives and secret feelings to all Veronica's remarks, for the only reason that they were friends.

And even that had been an act.

The studio had insisted that Veronica and Cora spend time together, so Cora's straight-laced reputation could make Veronica more proper, back when the studio considered such things important.

"I'll be fine," Cora said.

"You always were an odd thing," Veronica said. "Very well. Most of the servants went to the village. They don't want to hang around here, and since the weather is nice, we didn't stop them."

"That's fine," Cora said.

"Very well," Veronica said breezily and waved goodbye.

Cora headed down the corridor to Lady Audrey's room at once and knocked on the door.

"Come in," Lady Audrey said cheerfully, and Cora entered.

"Miss Clarke!" A flicker of surprise seemed to pass over Lady Audrey's face.

Lady Audrey was in dark, wide-legged trousers and a flowing cream-colored blouse. Her hair was tied up out of her way. Her face was red, and paint splattered her clothes.

"I'm sorry to disturb you," Cora said.

"What is it?" Lady Audrey said uncertainly.

Cora regretted how passionately Randolph and she had followed her when she'd attempted to go home. "Can you help me? I-I need a gramophone."

Her eyes filled with suspicion for a moment, but then she nodded. "Yes. My parents have one. We can visit Oak Manor. It's really quite close." Lady Audrey grinned. "Besides, there must be some advantage to not having Mr. Hall scowling at us when we strode too near the foyer."

Cora nodded, and guilt moved through her. "We may have been overly hasty in locking him up."

Lady Audrey paused and scrutinized her. "Men can mislead one."

"Naturally," Cora said quickly, as if to adopt some of the worldliness Lady Audrey seemed to possess. "But Randolph—"

"Is certainly a suspect."

"You're right," Cora admitted, but Lady Audrey did not look boastful.

"It's difficult," Lady Audrey said. "I understand. And perhaps Randolph is not the killer."

Cora nodded, clasping the record more tightly to her.

"After all these horrible deaths," Lady Audrey continued, "it would be dreadful if the police were to arrest the wrong person."

They strode through the corridors, down the stairs and into the foyer.

"It's so quiet here," Cora remarked.

"One of their own died this time."

Lady Audrey and Cora put on their various fortifications against the cold and departed the manor house.

The gray sky had turned a brilliant blue, and all the world sparkled. The sun glowed, and its bright rays illuminated each icy branch, each crystal-covered statue, and even each glistening block of ice in the moat with such vigor, as if to boast of nature's earlier prowess at having created the blizzard. Some snow settled on them in places, though they could not mask the glare of the sun's reflection on the ice. The snow sparkled under the sunlight, and the wind had swept it into pleasing shapes, as if seeking to bring nature nearer the heavens. It seemed impossible to dwell on any negative consequences of the storm, even though the manor house had been as isolated as if they'd been barricaded by the best army.

"It's so lovely," Cora breathed.

"Yes," Lady Audrey said. "There's not a murder here every day."

Cora nodded. The sun shone brightly through the trees, as if life was wonderful, as if no one had died at all. Perhaps she should return inside. She was likely wrong. Surely Veronica couldn't really have murdered her father-in-law. But the thought didn't feel right. It seemed to twist its way into her stomach.

Because, of everyone Cora had ever known, wasn't Veronica perhaps the least unexpected person? Veronica had strong opinions. She'd clawed her way to the top of Hollywood, all in perfect manicures. She'd stormed British society, toppling the various rules of decorum that suggested a future duke should only marry a debutante. The skills an English woman was supposed to have to become a good wife to an aristocrat included a knowledge of tableware and ability to make benign conversation, instead of an ability to acquire worldwide renown.

It didn't help that Veronica had lately excelled at playing vamps, happy to accept roles playing femme fatales, helped by the columnists' frequent mention of her as displaying disastrous behavior.

The duke had threatened her. Could Cora truly say that Veronica would have held onto loftier values in the face of his contempt and urge to destroy all she'd made for herself?

Cora wanted to say yes.

She wanted so badly to say yes.

But Veronica had had the gramophone. She'd had the opportunity. She'd had the means. And she'd been in possession of an excellent motive.

It didn't matter how pleasant Veronica might be if she didn't see one as a threat.

If Veronica had taken two lives—well, Cora would have to inform someone.

Gladys had been young. Joyous. She hadn't engaged in nefarious activities such as selling weapons to Germany's allies, uncaring if they used them against England, uncaring even if they used them against their own people.

"The house is not far away," Lady Audrey said. "We can grab snowshoes.

I do love the countryside."

"Perhaps you should move here," Cora said.

Lady Audrey smiled. "Perhaps I shall."

After a short distance they came to another manor house. It was less grand than Chalcroft Park, with neither turrets nor a moat, but it looked older and perhaps even more elegant. It had long windows that cast lovely light into the house when they entered.

Cora's shoulders relaxed. "This is splendid."

"The gramophone is in the parlor," Lady Audrey said. "I'll show it to you."

Cora followed her into the room and put on the radio play.

"I'll make some tea," Lady Audrey said, leaving.

Cora settled down on the sofa and listened carefully to the play.

Perhaps it had been a silly idea.

There was mostly conversation.

Lady Audrey arrived with tea. "Mind if I listen?"

"Oh, go ahead," Cora said.

Lady Audrey poured the tea into blue and white china cups. "Just why did you want to play this record?"

"It's just a hunch," Cora admitted. "I don't think I can share yet."

"You think the new Lady Holt had something to do with the murder?"

Cora widened her eyes.

"I recognize the name of the record," Lady Audrey said. "We discussed it at dinner."

"Oh, so we did." Cora nodded and continued to listen to the radio play.

There was a part on the record where the person went into a basement. It took a while for him to scream, but when he did—it was dreadful.

She'd been correct.

Unfortunately.

Lady Audrey flinched at the scream. "I should make some more tea. I don't need to hear the person discovering a body in the basement."

Cora jerked her head toward Lady Audrey. "How did you know that he discovered a body?"

Lady Audrey faltered, and tea spilled over the saucer. Her face flushed, and she set down the tea and saucer onto the coffee table abruptly. The porcelain clattered noisily over the marble table. "What did you say?"

Cora frowned. "How did you know he'd discovered a body?"

"It's—er—obvious."

"He could have been stabbed. Or shot. Or drowned."

"I know methods of killing people," Lady Audrey said impatiently. "I-I must have heard it."

"You said you never heard the radio play before," Cora said. "In the radio play we don't know *why* he was screaming. In the next scene the narrator tells us the reason."

Lady Audrey flushed. "I-I heard it before. I-I don't like admitting to listening to crime dramas. Might not work with my intellectual reputation."

"Or perhaps you didn't want to give Veronica the satisfaction of knowing that her project is a big deal?"

"That's it," Lady Audrey said. "I was jealous. You understand, surely."

Cora took her tea and sipped it slowly.

The scream had been there.

Veronica could have put on the gramophone when she changed, turning up the volume for the quiet part, and then waited for the scream to sound. Perhaps she'd opened the window so everyone could be sure to hear the scream better, or perhaps simply so people could think that an intruder had murdered him, should people not believe that a chandelier had crushed him.

It was dreadful.

Veronica must have been desperate for the duke to not threaten her to divorce her husband.

Cora frowned.

But it did seem...unlike her.

Still, this explained how the murder could have happened.

But perhaps... Perhaps Lady Audrey had done the same thing.

But why would Lady Audrey have gone through all the trouble of doing that?

Lady Audrey had been in her room when the murder happened.

She didn't have an alibi.

The only people who had an alibi were Mr. Ardingley and Edmund.

Edmund.

The new duke.

The man who inherited his father's fortune and title.

The man whom the duke had desired she marry.

Would Lady Audrey have protected him?

They were childhood neighbors.

Had Lady Audrey wanted there to be more between them?

Had Edmund?

She looked out Lady Audrey's bedroom window.

A figure in black strode toward them.

A figure whose hair looked very much like Edmund's.

"Is that the duke?" Cora asked, her voice wobbling.

A smile flickered on Lady Audrey's face. "Oh, yes."

Cora stepped away from the window.

It seemed odd that he'd followed them here.

If there was just something that he needed them to be informed of, surely he could have sent word to them without physically stopping by.

There were advantages to being a duke after all.

A chill went through Cora.

Veronica had never liked the relationship between Lady Audrey and her husband. She said they'd been far too close, even as children.

Edmund was handsome in his way.

Did he perhaps really love Lady Audrey after all? Or had they simply been working together to ensure he received his full inheritance?

I shouldn't be here.

Horror rushed through Cora.

She was all alone in a strange place.

No one knew she was here.

Lady Audrey slipped down the stairs to greet Edmund, and Cora peered out the window.

They were leaning far too close.

Almost as if they were—kissing.

Who would have better access to Veronica's gramophone than the duke?

Who else would be able to know about the record she'd brought of the radio play?

Why, they'd even played the radio play on the BBC—perhaps the duke had heard the lengthy scream on that. Heavens, perhaps Lady Audrey had.

All Cora had achieved by coming here was informing Lady Audrey that she knew about the record.

And now she'd seen Edmund.

They'd killed twice before.

Why would they hesitate to kill a third time?

Cora tried to remain nonchalant when he went up the steps.

If they thought she didn't suspect them, perhaps they could let her get away.

If only Randolph were with her.

If only she hadn't been so horribly wrong.

Chapter Twenty-seven

Cora dashed across the drawing room and settled onto the sofa. She grabbed hold of the tea and did her best to feign innocence.

Footsteps approached, and her heartbeat quickened. She focused on the dove blue painted walls and long white curtains that seemed to embody calm. The portraits of pastel-wearing women that hung on the walls, presumably of Lady Audrey's ancestors, seemed to be of people who'd never read about an unpleasant occurrence, much less commit murder.

"Hello." Cora forced her voice to sound casual. "Tea?"

"Lady Audrey told me you found a certain record," Edmund said.

"So I did. A mystery. It was—er—most entertaining."

"And why did you choose to listen to that?"

Cora attempted to shrug casually. "I wanted something diverting. Music can be so tiring after a while."

"Don't waste my time. You know Audrey and I were behind the recent murders. You know we used the gramophone to give me an alibi."

Oh.

Lady Audrey had told Edmund everything.

Cora set down her teacup.

Fear prickled every nerve in her body.

What was he going to do to her?

Stab her and then shove her body in one of these chimneys?

"You wanted your inheritance," Cora said.

He scoffed. "It wasn't just about the money. But I'm a duke now. It's a very splendid thing."

"He was your father," Cora exclaimed. "How could you have murdered him?"

Edmund laughed. "You are really too sentimental. You would think you would be somewhat more hardened. Still believing those Victorian fantasies generated by authors decades ago." He snorted. "My *father* was nothing to me. His health was holding me back. He could have lived for twenty more years, frail, pitiful, threatening to cut me off at any moment."

"He was going to see the solicitor next month," Cora said.

"He told me. Foolish man."

"So you murdered him," Cora said. "And you used Veronica's gramophone to confuse the time of death."

"Yes," Edmund said. "I thought that was quite a clever touch. She'd told me the name of the radio show, and that she was listening to the record. As if I was interested in it. But when I decided to murder him...well, it seemed like a good idea in case the accident idea wasn't believed. If they suspected anyone, it would be her. Once they found out about her pitiful childhood. Father told me all about it."

"Quite revolting," Lady Audrey sniffed. "It's a wonder she was allowed to become a star. There are higher standards in England, thank goodness. I wouldn't mind seeing her hang. It was a mistake for darling Edmund to marry her. If only he'd listened to everyone. But we can rectify things now. We can marry. Just how it's supposed to be."

Edmund swept into a bow and kissed her hand. "Yes, darling."

His eyes though were lifeless, and Cora shivered.

She doubted he cared for Lady Audrey either.

She doubted his regard extended to anyone besides himself.

"Why did you kill the maid?"

"She discovered Edmund and me in bed together one morning before Veronica and you arrived. If she told someone else... If she used her mind..."

Oh.

Gladys had mentioned that Lady Audrey had given her information about the murder. She must have visited Lady Audrey's room. The maids split which rooms they attended, but Gladys must have served Lady Audrey. And of course, she would have noticed if Edmund had been there one morning but known she wasn't supposed to share that information.

That was the gossip that Gladys had been unsure whether to share with Veronica.

One shouldn't speak poorly of one's employer.

Servants were trusted to be discreet. No wonder she had been so torn.

"After I left the library, I heard her talk with you. Thank goodness Wexley chased her away. It was easy to send her on an errand upstairs and then kill her."

"And why did you leave her in my room?"

"Well. I would have liked another location. No one would believe that you desired to kill your maid. She was a horrible one, but you hadn't known her long. But I knew you were occupied downstairs, and you wouldn't even know something was wrong when you didn't see her in the evening."

"And why did you use the strap from Mr. Hall's camera?"

"I thought that was a nice touch," Lady Audrey said. "Personally I think anyone entering a house in a blizzard is suspicious, especially when they have the gall to begin questioning people. I didn't expect you to actually accuse him of murder. We couldn't believe our luck."

Edmund grinned. "I wonder how we should murder you."

Cora's heartbeat raced. "Y-you can't do that."

"I assure you we can." Lady Audrey's eyes flickered. "Two bodies in two days. Nobody suspected us. You even suspected your own friend and your-would-be lover, rather than us."

"I suspected you. I suspected everyone!"

But Lady Audrey was right. Cora had been so determined to see justice fulfilled that she'd stopped following her instincts. She'd stopped trusting in general. Her job had been snatched away, and she had been uncertain about anything, not knowing what to believe of absolutely anyone.

I was wrong.

"If there's a third death, on your estate this time, I'm sure more attention will be drawn to you, especially since you are not with the others," Cora said. "They might even suspect you."

"Stop talking," Edmund grumbled. His wrist wobbled as he raked his hand through his hair. "My head hurts."

Cora didn't feel sorry for him, no matter how stressful a task Edmund found murder to be. Surely, any concept of good and evil one had been taught during one's life might cause one to waver. Edmund knew murder was wrong. Likely the prospect of a noose coming down on his throat if he left too blatant a clue accidentally for someone to find was similarly nerve-wracking.

"Let's take the sleigh." Lady Audrey pulled Cora up and ushered her from the splendor of the manor house to the frigid winter air. "Get inside."

Cora climbed into the sleigh, and it soon moved over the snow. The horses' bells jingled merrily, uncaring that they might as well be taking her to the underworld. Their manes still glistened, and the world was still beautiful.

The sleigh rushed toward the manor house, and the turrets came into view. Where was a stone for the sleigh to get stuck on?

But there was nothing.

Perhaps not even hope.

Had Edmund and Lady Audrey been evil all their lives, or had the temptation to kill simply overwhelmed them?

Had Edmund desired to become a duke so badly? Had the prospect of all the money, all the magazines that would praise him for his attractiveness and his kindheartedness simply for giving the occasional charitable donation and cutting ribbons on buildings that would bear his name, overwhelmed him and compelled him to hasten his father's death?

Cora tried to think.

What would she have done in the *Gal Detective* films?

In movies, the victim tried to always keep the murderer speaking until help arrived.

I might not survive.

Her heart leaped unevenly in her chest, and she swallowed hard, as if the action might force the panic down.

"I don't understand," Cora said, striving to keep her voice calm. "Why would you have killed your own father?"

Edmund waved his hand dismissively. "You wouldn't understand."

"He was your own flesh and blood."

"Americans, for all their boast of power, seem remarkably prone to provincialism and excessive sentiment." Edmund assessed her, and Cora tried to find something in his face that would explain his actions, but he appeared every bit as good-natured and mild-mannered as before. "Look, he never wanted to be a father. It was his duty, and he delayed it to the ripe old age of forty."

"So your father may not have had longstanding paternal instincts."

"No," Edmund said. "He didn't have *any* paternal desires."

"That's not a reason to kill him."

"Signor Palombi was there. He was my mother's lover. He was going to tell the duke that I'm his child. That I'm a bastard and cannot inherit from him!"

Cora blinked. "I don't think that was Signor Palombi's intention. Why did you think Signor Palombi was your father? Did your mother tell you that?"

"No," Edmund said. "But it's obvious. Rhys resembled the duke much more than I ever did."

"Your father was still a person," she said, struggling to understand why Edmund had taken his life. "Perhaps you didn't like him, but how could you murder him?"

Lady Audrey grinned. "We live in the countryside. We've been shooting rabbits and foxes since we were little. A bit of blood doesn't befuddle us."

"The man was poised to destroy my life," Edmund grumbled. "Why can't you see that I had to kill him?"

His voice rose, like an irate toddler, and Lady Audrey stroked his shoulder.

"You had to do it," Lady Audrey said in a soothing tone, and Edmund relaxed under her administrations.

"Why did you marry Veronica?" Cora asked abruptly.

"You do have *so* many questions," Lady Audrey said.

"Who else are you going to tell? Perhaps it might help to talk about it."

"Lest it plague our dreams?" Edmund snorted. "Please, not all of us are followers of Viennese quacks."

Cora was silent.

She was hardly a Freud enthusiast.

She knew too little about him to have a strong opinion.

But even if she were a devotee of the man who had recently inspired film directors to add nightmare sequences to their movies and have their camera dwell on strange symbols, she would not care if Edmund and Lady Audrey were plagued for the rest of their sleeping hours with sinister images of chandeliers and staircases.

She had to believe that she could escape and that any knowledge from their confessions could lead to their conviction.

Because if this really was to be the end of her life—and she abhorred to admit that it might be—she was not going to spend her last minutes alive devoid of hope.

And after all, if she did escape, she needed to ensure that they were not acquitted by a jury intimidated by Edmund's and Lady Audrey's lofty aristocratic background and perhaps confused why two people who seemed to have everything would end the lives of others with a casual cruelty that others confined to squashing insects.

"I thought people would be impressed that I'd married a star," Edmund said stiffly. "But people weren't impressed. They were appalled that she's American. Appalled that she didn't know anyone in British high society. They said she'd caught me instead of the other way around."

A wave of irritation swept through Cora. "You did make a good catch. Veronica is Hollywood royalty. She's clever and talented and beautiful and—"

Lady Audrey's face whitened. "Don't pay attention to her," she said to Edmund. "She's Veronica's best friend. Naturally she would be biased."

Edmund nodded uneasily.

Cora was struck by how weak Edmund was, how easily swayed.

Was that the personality that the late duke despised? Had Lady Audrey used him for her purposes, ensuring that he would inherit a dukedom and abandon his wife in order for her to become a duchess?

"Why did you help him?" Cora asked Lady Audrey.

Lady Audrey closed her eyes. Snowflakes fell onto her lashes. The pristine color seemed at odds with an imagination that had plotted two deaths and likely had already construed a premature end for Cora herself.

"Love," Lady Audrey said simply. She smirked. "But you wouldn't understand. You accused your love interest of murder and had him locked in a tower."

Edmund chuckled. "We didn't expect that. That was good news for us."

Lady Audrey joined his laughter, and for a moment, they seemed every bit as doting as any couple, one whose conversations were devoted

to news items and pleasantries from their days, rather than carrying out vile murders during the time in which they were not in each other's arms.

"I wasn't the only person who suspected him," Cora huffed. "He was suspicious. And he's not my love interest."

"You mean, you haven't bedded him yet?" Lady Audrey gave a languid stretch. "How delightfully dull. I was under the impression that American prudishness was a Midwestern phenomenon and didn't stretch to the Pacific. But I suppose Los Angeles is small compared to cosmopolitan London."

Cora pressed her lips together. "Don't insult Los Angeles."

Lady Audrey and Edmund chuckled.

"Well, it was a trifle inconvenient that you crowned Randolph the murderer," Lady Audrey said. "That honor was supposed to belong to Veronica."

"That's why you used her gramophone and record," Cora said.

Veronica had been right. She would have been accused.

"A divorce is less scandal inducing than a hanging, even if it is generally more expensive," Edmund said.

"You would go through a divorce?" Cora asked. "That hardly seems proper."

"People will laud his good sense," Lady Audrey said quickly, shooting Cora a warning glance. "Besides, likely Edmund will be able to get an annulment. The duke did the most helpful research into that process before he died."

"So what do you mean to do?" Cora asked. "Tie me up to a tree?"

"No." Lady Audrey's eyes flashed. "The moat is frozen—but not entirely. And everyone knows her attempt to ski was pitiful."

She gave a cruel laugh, and Cora bristled.

"A not-too-clever American," Lady Audrey said, "might be confused. She might think she could cut across the moat. It would be tragic. But not impossible."

"They wouldn't think that," Cora said.

But she knew in her heart that they would.

She'd seen the moat.

If they threw her into a hole in the ice... She shivered. She was already cold. And to be plunged into icy water, struggling to get back out. Her heart tightened.

"Somebody may witness it," Cora said.

"I doubt it. They were eager to leave. And if anyone sees anything, they'll think we were trying to rescue you."

"You can confess," Cora said. "You might go to jail..."

"We would hang," Edmund said. "No, I assure you. We will certainly not confess to anything. We can bear the brunt of any guilt."

"I assure you we won't feel much," Lady Audrey said. "You needn't comfort yourself by imagining us tortured for the rest of our lives. We'll have money and lovely titles."

"But you," Cora said. "How can you be with this man who just murders people?"

Lady Audrey laughed. "They were my ideas."

Edmund squeezed her hand.

"My advice has gotten more complicated since the duke asked me for help as a child on how to build a tree house, but I still provide it."

"My darling," Edmund said, and Cora's stomach tensed.

The castle turrets were in view.

Chapter Twenty-eight

Edmund halted the sleigh and tied the horses to a tree.

"Come on, Miss Clarke," Lady Audrey said. "We're going on a walk. Enjoy the pleasant view. It will be the last thing you see."

Randolph.

Randolph was locked in the manor house.

His room should overlook them. He was locked in...but the place did have windows. Could he climb out?

Cora told herself she was being ridiculous.

Of course he couldn't help her.

"Randolph!" Cora shouted, unwilling to give up, as they neared the manor house.

"Be quiet." Lady Audrey slapped her. Her look was icy, as if striving to resemble the ice in the perilous moat. "I think it's time for your fall."

Sharp wind swept over Cora. She was wearing a coat and she was already freezing.

Perhaps she could run.

Yes.

She could run.

There were two of them, but she would have to try.

She jumped from the sleigh and into the snow.

Her legs burned, and her feet slid on the slick ground.

The snow was so heavy.

Heavens.

This was utterly dreadful.

And not working.

She heard footsteps and curses behind her.

"Get her," Lady Audrey yelled.

Cora's heart sped, and she struggled on this new terrain.

She'd only seen snow for the first time this week.

And now she was rushing about in it.

The snow reached past her knees. The ground was not sturdy, and she moved far too slowly.

In the next moment, she felt strong arms reach against her. She was lifted up and was being carried toward the moat.

"Randolph!" Cora screamed again, hoping against hope. "Help!"

A gloved hand covered her mouth.

She looked desperately for a servant, but everyone had left.

No one was going to rescue her.

Just like no one had rescued Gladys.

And no one had rescued the duke who'd died in his own bed, at the hand of his own son.

Cora kept her eyes open.

Was this the last light she would see?

The last snow, the last sky, the last wall, the last—

The last moment of life.

Her heart continued to race, and then she flew through the air and plunged into icy water.

She struggled to swim despite her heavy coat.

The water stung her eyes. She tried to see, tried to orient herself.

It must be so dirty—though that was the least of her concerns.

Her lungs burned. She needed air.

She tried to swim up—but where was the surface?

Panic flayed through her. There was only ice around her.

Her lungs—

Cora moved up, breaking through the surface.

It was air.

She inhaled, gasping, but in the next moment, a hand pushed her back into the water.

This was it, this was the end.

A splash sounded in the distance.

Poor Randolph would hang for the murder of Gladys and the Duke of Hawley if they didn't decide to continue framing Veronica.

Horror rushed through her, and once again, her lungs burned.

There was no hope.

She needed to get free.

She needed to warn them.

She kicked hard, trying to find her way to the surface, but she was so tired, so cold, her lungs ached, and—

A strong hand grabbed onto Cora.

She was being dragged up to the surface, toward the light, toward life itself.

She broke through the barrier, dodging the floating ice.

Cora inhaled.

"I have you," a voice said.

"Randolph?"

"What do you think you are doing?" Edmund said.

"Rescuing her," Randolph said. "You animal."

In the next moment, Randolph struck Edmund on his jaw, and they tumbled into the snow together.

Cora's heart raced. Where was Lady Audrey?

She was approaching.

Rushing to stop them.

Rushing to help her lover.

Cora wasn't going to let that happen.

With all her remaining strength, Cora yanked hold of Lady Audrey's leg and pulled her downward.

She was still coughing, still sputtering—and now Lady Audrey was on top of her.

That was perhaps a mistake.

Lady Audrey was strong, and iron arms gripped around Cora's body.

Cora was still disoriented from the experience of being submerged in the icy moat.

She'd thought she was going to die.

Cora was too close to the moat now, and she struggled against her assailant.

"Help," Cora screamed. "Help!"

"What on earth is this racket?" a new voice boomed.

Wexley.

Hope rushed through Cora.

"Thank goodness you're here," Edmund said. "This man escaped."

"No!" Cora exclaimed. "The duke is the murderer!"

"Nonsense—" Edmund said, but Randolph took the opportunity to strike a blow to the duke's jaw.

"That's enough." The butler strolled into the snow, not seeming to mind that his livery was being destroyed.

He yanked Randolph away from Edmund.

"Inside. Both of you. *Now.*" The butler glowered at them. "We are going to wait for the police to arrive."

"Yes," Edmund said. "Thank you. I'll go see if I can find them." He jerked a finger at Randolph. "This man needs to be locked up again."

"No," Cora shrieked again.

"I can explain everything," Randolph said.

The butler removed a pistol and directed it at them. "I don't know whom to believe."

"Wexley!" Edmund said, clearly shocked. "Is that one of my pistols?"

The butler blushed. "Forgive me, your grace, but after poor Gladys's murder it occurred to me that I would feel rather safer with that in my breast pocket."

"But you stole."

"Borrowed," Wexley said. "And we are still on the premises."

"Well, stop pointing it at *me*," Edmund sputtered.

Wexley retained a steady grip on the pistol. "I'm sorry, your grace. But I'm not going to take anyone's side without knowing all the facts."

"That does make sense," Lady Audrey said smoothly. "Would you like me to fetch the police? Obviously I would never have killed anyone." She laughed.

"Don't believe her," Cora said quickly.

"I won't," Wexley said. "Miss Clarke, please change from those wet clothes. And bring blankets for everyone."

Cora nodded and hurried away, her teeth chattering fiercely.

Finally, after what seemed like hours, but could not have been long, the others arrived.

"What's going on here?" Veronica asked, entering the foyer.

"I am afraid that your husband is a murderer," Cora said.

"Nonsense, darling." Veronica smiled. "Tell her it's nonsense."

"Of course it is," Edmund said.

"I beg to differ," Randolph said.

Veronica frowned. "Why is your hair wet, Cora? You didn't even want to go outside and now you seemed to have gone swimming?"

"Your husband pushed her in the water," Randolph said.

"You don't tend to be clumsy, Edmund," Veronica said.

"It was an intentional push," Cora said, her voice breaking.

Veronica stopped. "You're being serious?"

"He killed Gladys and his father, and when he knew I'd found out—he wanted to kill me."

"But—"

For once in her life, Veronica seemed entirely devoid of words.

"Lady Audrey was his accomplice," Randolph said.

Mr. Ardingley narrowed his eyes. "Wexley, I can direct this gun at him. I always knew I was the better son."

"Perhaps you might find some rope to tie him up with, sir," Wexley suggested.

Mr. Ardingley grinned. "You're a good man."

Soon both Lady Audrey and Edmund were tied up.

"How could you have killed your own father?" the dowager duchess asked. "What could possess you?"

Edmund scowled. "Don't carry on lying, Mother. I know he's not my real father. I know Signor Palombi is truly my father."

"My darling boy," said the dowager duchess. "The duke *was* your father."

"Nonsense," Edmund said. "You can tell me."

"But it's true."

"I know that Signor Palombi was your lover," Edmund said. "I saw a picture of him in your room."

The dowager blinked. "You went through my private things?"

"I was suspicious. You were so happy to see him. You're never happy about anything."

"But you didn't read the back of the photograph?"

"It's not my fault you never taught me Czech," Edmund said.

"I imagine your father is regretting his decision to not let me do so," Lady Denisa said the dowager. "Mr. Palombi and I are relations. We have recently rekindled our acquaintanceship, but I assure you that there is nothing romantic about it."

"But you spoke in private."

"About our country." The dowager swallowed. "Recent news has made me nostalgic. Our country is sadly fragmenting. Yes, I invited him for Christmas, but only because I couldn't stand the thought of him spending Christmas alone in a new country in a hotel."

"And why pretend to be Italian?" Edmund asked.

The dowager and Signor Palombi glanced at each other. Cora wondered how much they might share.

"I left Czechoslovakia years ago, and so did my *cousin,*" explained the dowager duchess.

Edmund's face paled, and his mother's shoulders seemed to relax.

"Archibald enjoyed the open space here," Signor Palombi said.

Mrs. Ardingley frowned. "He made good use of the hallways."

Mr. Ardingley raised his eyebrows.

"One notices the floor in great detail when one is compelled to wheel oneself on top of it," Mrs. Ardingley murmured.

"I'm glad those days are behind you." Mr. Ardingley kissed the top of his wife's head.

Mrs. Ardingley's brother-in-law might just have committed two gruesome murders, but that did not seem to encroach upon the rekindling of her relationship with the murderer's brother.

Perhaps one day things can truly be normal again.

"Wait." Edmund blinked several times, and his Adam's apple moved up and down rapidly, as if his throat had been drained of all moisture. "You mean to say," he said, his voice breaking, though he barreled on, "that I murdered my own father."

"Yes, my child," said his mother.

"And he wasn't going to take away my inheritance?"

"He never mentioned it."

"It was the right thing to do, darling," Lady Audrey said. "We were so close to being together forever. And you would have had the money so much sooner."

"My late husband was not in good health," the dowager said. "You should have let him live."

Edmund raked a hand through his hair. "Oh, Lord."

"Prayers will hardly work." Mrs. Ardingley sniffed. "I cannot believe you would have behaved so appallingly. After that expensive education too! How tragic that the duke never learned how superior my husband was to you."

"I'm sure he knew at the end, my dear." Mr. Ardingley squeezed his wife's hand.

Edmund's face seemed to turn a shade of green.

Cora wondered what sort of dubious deals with Germany had been halted because of Edmund's action. Perhaps Edmund had unwittingly aided various resistance movements against the rapidly rising National Socialists.

"I'm sorry," Edmund murmured.

"You almost killed me," Cora said. "You tried very hard to kill me. And you did kill Gladys."

"The maid?" Edmund shrugged. "She wasn't important."

"Because she wasn't a family member?"

"Because she was a servant," Edmund said, shaking his head. "These Americans."

"She didn't deserve to die," his mother admonished.

Edmund shrugged. "Her death is inconsequential. No problems will be caused by her absence. If anything, it will give the housekeeper a chance to hire someone more appropriate."

"She was a sweet girl," Veronica said, and then sighed. "A true fan."

"As if you didn't find her irritating," Lady Audrey said. "Far too talkative."

The duchess frowned. "I will not tolerate you spending the rest of your time tarnishing that poor girl's memory."

"And yet you had another maid. It's not tarnishing when it's the truth," Edmund said valiantly, and Lady Audrey smiled, her gaze somehow managing to remain adoring.

"I've had my lady's maid for years," the duchess said regally. "A fact of which you are well aware, and which you should not choose to conveniently forget. That girl left her family to serve in our large, luxurious manor house. It is an experience that I can relate to, for I came here from Czechoslovakia without my family so many years ago. It will always be a sorrow to me that she was treated so poorly here. One might be nervous about going down a dark alleyway in a neighborhood known for its proclivity for crime, but one hardly expects one's employer to strangle one with a camera strap."

Edmund's cheeks flamed. "I'm sorry, Mother."

"It's too late," she said softly. "I didn't teach you the difference between right or wrong well enough."

"That boy was sent away to school when he was seven," Mr. Ardingley said sternly. "I will not have you berate yourself."

"That's sweet of you," the dowager said.

"I am not dead yet. You'll have plenty of time to talk amongst yourselves as if I'm not here, once I'm *actually* not here." Edmund set his face into a scowl. "Look. Perhaps I was callous. But I would never have killed Gladys if I didn't have to."

"And why did you have to?" his mother asked. "Was Gladys brandishing some frightful weapon, vowing to use you as target practice?"

Edmund blinked. "What? Of course not."

"She found out about our love," Lady Audrey said smoothly.

"Caught you in the act?" Mr. Ardingley said. "Did she have a camera? Was she threatening to send the images to the tabloids?"

"Of course not," Edmund sputtered. "Maids don't carry cameras. Their hands are occupied with other materials. The—er—cleaning sort."

There was an awkward pause while the others waited to see if he would elaborate, though evidently Edmund's Harrow and Oxford education had not extended to the development of a vocabulary for cleaning supplies.

"But she still could have mentioned it to someone," Edmund said. "And that would have—er—been suspicious."

Mr. Ardingley laughed. "You never did get around much. The policemen wouldn't have wasted the energy to raise a single eyebrow. They rather expect us to be Dionysian men, not that they would term it that, whether we wanted to be or not." He kissed his wife's hand. "Some of us do not delight in such experiences."

Cora tilted her head and assessed them. It was hard to see Mr. Ardingley as a devoted husband, but perhaps he was simply bored with the role of playing an non-devoted one.

Mrs. Ardingley still seemed suspicious, but Cora noted that she did smile when Mr. Ardingley kissed her hand.

Perhaps Mrs. Ardingley's sacrifice had awakened something inside Mr. Ardingley. Cora hoped for both their sakes that it lasted.

Her gaze found Randolph, and she drew back, embarrassed. He'd saved her life, but the encounter they'd had before he'd flung himself into an icy moat from a turret had been when she'd accused him of two murders.

He was bound to hold her in suspicion. Certainly, he would hardly be sending her the sort of besotted glances that Mr. Ardingley was sending Mrs. Ardingley.

Cora's chest hurt, as the now familiar guilt moved through her, sending pain through her body with expertise.

A dark vehicle moved slowly over the snow, sliding over the ice.

"That must be the English police," Signor Palombi said.

"They are positively creeping," Lady Audrey said disdainfully and pulled on her constraints.

"You're not going anywhere," Mr. Ardingley said, crossing his arms. "You killed my father."

Lady Audrey blinked and looked away.

"Perhaps you can donate your Rolls Royce to the police department," Mrs. Ardingley said sweetly. "You won't be using it ever again."

Lady Audrey's face whitened, but she turned toward Edmund. "Good bye, my darling."

Her features froze.

Edmund wasn't looking at her.

He was looking at Veronica.

"Good bye," he murmured to her.

Golly.

Edmund didn't even care for Lady Audrey. He'd second guessed his relationship with Veronica, after the papers and his friends had mocked it.

Finally, the vehicle pulled up, and a man in a uniform exited.

It was the constable.

The same one they'd met at the station.

Constable Kirby.

"What's going on here?" Kirby asked.

"My husband and one of my maids have been murdered," the dowager duchess said in her most regal voice.

Kirby frowned. "I was hoping it was a prank call."

"One does not jest about such things." The dowager duchess sniffed and flung her fur stole around her shoulders again.

"Don't you worry, your grace," the constable said. "I'll find the murderer. I've packed my bag." He snapped it open and pulled out a magnifying glass and a pair of gloves. We won't let the murderer run free. Not in this village."

"We've already determined who the murderers are," the dowager informed him.

"Murderers?" the constable gasped. "Multiple ones?"

"Two. But yes. This young lady solved the case. The murderers were my son and my former neighbor, Lady Audrey."

"Are you sure?"

"Unfortunately, yes," Lady Denisa said. "I think you'll find the courts will agree."

"Well, then." The constable took out a pair of handcuffs. "I only brought one pair," he said mournfully.

"We've improvised." Mr. Ardingley pointed to the rope.

"Right. Good." The constable took out a book, flipped through the pages and put on a pair of glasses. "My first arrest. I'm honored I can do it before you, your grace."

"Hurry up," Mr. Ardingley said.

The constable's face grew ruddy, and after reading them the relevant page, he soon hauled them to the police car.

Cora watched the dark car move down the hill, and for the first time she allowed herself a small sigh of relief.

Chapter Twenty-nine

A somber mood had overtaken the group after Edmund and Lady Audrey were ushered off by the constable and the others dispersed. Cora returned to her room. Her legs still felt unsteady, the memory of being thrust into the icy moat still imprinted on them. Cora drew herself a bath and sank into the warm water, trying not to conjure up images of the moat. She didn't linger in the water and soon dressed.

She was alive.

Joy cascaded through her, even as she clutched hold of the woolen blanket she'd been given.

How marvelous that she had not succumbed in the moat.

If Veronica hadn't gone back to Hollywood to finalize things, if she'd stayed with her husband, would nothing have changed? If Edmund's father had not despised her and hadn't threatened Edmund with removing him from his will, would things have changed?

Was Edmund evil? If he hadn't killed the duke, would he have killed someone else later on—for example, Veronica?

Or could all of this have been avoided?

Cora hadn't truly believed in evil.

People had told her it existed, but it had seemed to be an abstract concept.

Yet she had seen the duke's murdered body and the maid.

The thing was...Edmund did not seem like a murderer.

He scowled at times, but he was not alone in that habit.

He also could be charming and he talked pleasantly on a whole manner of subjects.

And yet he'd murdered.

Not once, but twice.

Perhaps Veronica would always say that Lady Audrey had influenced him negatively, but at what point was the decision to murder simply in a person's psyche?

Was it something that any person could be persuaded to do, given sufficient pressures and temptations?

Edmund would be tried in court and in all likelihood hanged.

Cora didn't know if that would be a deterrent to keep other people from succumbing to their own peculiar combination of pressures and temptations that might lead them to such a dishonorable path, but at least he would not be able to harm anyone else.

Cora would have to content herself with that.

Randolph seemed comfortable amidst the grand furniture, now his hair was not slick with snow, and his suit was not speckled with dirt and hibiscus petals.

The man had evidently managed to take a bath as well, and he looked once again refreshed, as if he couldn't possibly have spent the afternoon battling for her life and his.

"I wanted to say goodbye," Randolph said. "Shall we walk outside?"

"Oh." She nodded and followed him through the heavy doors after they put on the appropriate outerwear. The sun glinted over the snow, and the breeze felt cool against her face. "How did you rescue me?"

"I heard your scream. You'd given me your Shakespeare volume, and I smashed it through the window. It made a good substitute for a brick." He frowned. "It must be at the bottom of the moat now."

"So you've also saved me from finishing it."

"Two birds with one stone."

She laughed.

"I could have escaped earlier," he said, "but I didn't like the idea of being on the run for the rest of my life."

"Shocking."

"You probably would have thought me even more suspicious if I'd broken from a tower and clambered down it like I was practicing for a role in some English pantomime."

"So instead you just lunged in."

"You seemed worth it."

His face was so near hers. Their conversation had somehow changed to become more serious, and the air seemed thicker, more magnificent.

To think that she'd accused him of murder.

When she owed her life to him.

"I should never have thought ill of you," she said.

He shrugged. "Don't worry. I was perhaps acting suspiciously when you first met me."

"Why were you hiding in the hibiscus plants? Were you really a private detective, scrounging up negative information on Veronica?"

"Certain people wanted me to see what the duke's plans were. They thought if I gained his confidence as a private investigator, I might gain access to his house. I was already in California for another matter when I received the assignment, and I thought some photos of Veronica's house might make me seem more realistic."

"Oh."

"The original private investigator had already sent the duke information on Veronica."

"So you're really not a photographer."

"No, lassie. And I didn't need to be locked in that turret." His eyes sparkled. "Though I intend to tease you about it."

"Oh?" Relief coursed through her, and she smiled at him.

"Yes." He nodded solemnly. "For a very long time."

She shivered under his gaze, and he grabbed hold of her hand. Thick woolen gloves might have separated their fingers, but the firmness of his grip could not be masked. Energy rushed through her body.

He pulled her nearer to him. His lips brushed against hers, and then their lips danced together.

Fire throttled through her, despite the icy chill.

It didn't matter that they were standing before a manor house where two people had been murdered. The killers were in prison, and Cora could concentrate on the feel of strong, supple lips against hers.

Archibald barked, and Cora and Randolph parted.

"May I speak with you, Miss Clarke?" Signor Palombi asked.

"Certainly," Cora said.

"I'll be inside, lassie," Randolph said, and Cora nodded.

"The police will soon be directing their questions to everyone," Signor Palombi said. "And I would prefer not to be here. It looks like Hitler might attempt to control Czechoslovakia, and I will do my utmost to stop it."

"I'm so sorry," Cora said.

"You should have Archibald," Signor Palombi said.

"Me?" Cora widened her eyes. "But I've never had a dog. Or a cat. Or even a lizard."

"Archibald is quite unlike a lizard," Signor Palombi said evenly. "He won't mind in the least if your lizard caretaking skills are mediocre."

"Nonexistent," Cora said.

Signor Palombi assessed her, and she wondered if he might change his mind after all. But then he waved his hand in a dismissive fashion. "No, you'll do quite well."

"A dog is a large responsibility."

"You've managed to show that you are responsible. Besides, I wouldn't give him to you if I suspected you wouldn't get along." His smile wobbled. "Actually, I might do just that. But with instructions on how to find another home for him. I can't take care of him. Not anymore. I must make *ze* travel."

Cora nodded. Signor Palombi made no attempt at having an Italian accent now. He was Czech, and Czechoslovakia was in grave trouble. It's location and abundance of factories made it a good target for Germany, and Hitler had been speaking more and more about the supposed plight of those in the Sudetenland and the need to control it.

"My—er—employers won't let me have a dog. And as much as I would like to keep Archibald, if I had to choose—and I must—"

"You would choose your country," Cora finished. "I understand."

Signor Palombi nodded.

"And you mustn't worry," she said. "I will take care of him."

"A dog is a wonderful companion," Signor Palombi said. "But an Archibald—" He broke off, as if not knowing the English words that would most emphasize their relationship. "Why, it is spectacular."

Signor Palombi knelt on the ground.

Archibald moved toward him. He tilted his head toward Cora, as if flummoxed by Signor Palombi's position.

Sadness inundated Cora. Signor Palombi shouldn't have to give up his dog. Archibald shouldn't have to be parted from the man he'd shared his life with.

"Be a good boy." Signor Palombi stroked Archibald's coat, and the dog wagged his tail. "I would stay with you if I could, but I'm afraid I cannot."

Archibald seemed to assess him, as if attempting to interpret the seriousness of Signor Palombi's voice.

"Miss Clarke will take care of you now," Signor Palombi said. "You're going to belong to a starlet."

Archibald tilted his head up at Cora.

"You've always been a good boy," Signor Palombi said softly, and murmured some words in Czech.

The lump in Cora's throat thickened. "It's not fair."

"Perhaps not," Signor Palombi said, standing up. "And I could choose to do nothing. But there will be more people harmed than Archibald and me. I wish a separation from a dog was the worst that will happen, but I very much fear it will not be. You'll have to be brave too, miss Clarke. War is brewing, and not just for Czechoslovakia."

Cora scooped Archibald into her arms. He gazed at her uncertainly, but he still wagged his tail.

"Good," Signor Palombi said. "You'll get along fine. I was hoping you would agree. In fact—" He rustled through his coat and took out a piece of paper and unfolded it.

He handed it to her, and Cora noted the small, carefully printed letters. "You'll find everything you might need to know about Archibald there."

"Thank you."

Perhaps she'd never planned to have a dog, but everything had changed. She no longer was an actress in Hollywood, working sixteen-hour days. She could find a normal job. And she could care for Archibald.

She pressed his warm body against her chest. It would be nice to have company. Even the four-legged variety.

"Ah, Archibald's always been suspicious of strangers. He had a premonition about you."

Cora smiled, but Signor Palombi's face remained sober.

"He's very clever. He can be quite helpful. You'll see."

Cora nodded, startled.

A horn honked, and Signor Palombi sighed. "I suppose that's my taxi. I should go now."

"Good bye" Cora said.

"Good bye, young lady." Signor Palombi shook Archibald's paw solemnly and then departed.

Cora watched Signor Palombi's figure recede, and Archibald barked, perhaps realizing that something might not be quite right.

The taxi moved away from the manor house, and Archibald whimpered.

"It will be fine," Cora said, stroking the dog's curly coat.

Chapter Thirty

The next day, servants whisked her trunk downstairs. Perhaps they'd seen the Americans' arrival as bad luck, something the universe should never have allowed, and that it was not surprising their arrival had accompanied two deaths.

Murdered dukes had a habit of making the news, and a reporter had learned that she'd been thrust into the moat by the new duke.

A shot of Cora's figure was on every major newspaper.

Cora didn't want to think about how much Mr. Bellomo would despise the scandal.

She hadn't run off with some woman's husband, and she hadn't been arrested for drunk and disorderly behavior, but she had spent Christmas with a murderer.

It hadn't actually been the calm holiday Veronica had promised.

It seemed outrageous that the flowers could still look pretty in their vases, the petals still intact. It seemed ludicrous that mistletoe still dangled from the doors. The marriages in this home had been tainted by evil. And yet aristocrats still smiled placidly from their portraits in gilt frames.

The snow had halted, and no mist obscured the view.

The phone rang.

"The lines must be working again," somebody called out joyously.

"Excuse me," the butler said.

"Poor Wexley despises that invention," the dowager duchess said. "Door answering has always been sufficient frustration for him."

"Oh," Cora said.

A smile stole over the dowager's face. "You mustn't appear so shocked. He's quite gifted at other things, and I haven't seen such a regal glower since my days in Czechoslovakia. And sadly, the aristocrats there will not be doing that anytime soon."

"It is horrible about Hitler," Cora ventured.

"Indeed," said the dowager duchess. "And this country is not doing a single thing about it. Appeasement. Ha."

The butler appeared before Cora could respond to the dowager's remark. She had so many questions.

Back in Hollywood, war had seemed purely hypothetical, an excuse for stylists to put actors in uniforms, and on occasion, to smear their faces with dirt.

War was far more present here, perhaps because they'd so clearly suffered under the Great War. Middle-aged men were often not in possession of all their limbs.

People seemed alternatively eager to chide Chamberlain for not defending Europe's smaller countries from Hitler's greed to lauding Chamberlain's restraint and maintaining that Hitler was not so bad.

Cora hoped the latter was the case. That was Roosevelt's opinion, and she was proud of her president.

People might be so accustomed to viewing Germany negatively, given the number of people they'd killed for seemingly no reason in the last war, that it was natural for them to be suspicious of them now.

Maybe Hitler was correct. Perhaps the people in the smaller countries that bordered Germany desired to be part of Germany. Certainly, their economy was doing relatively well. Czechoslovakia was a new country; it had only been formed at the end of the Great War. It made sense that a country with more experience at governing might take better care of its people.

But Dowager Duchess Denisa seemed to view Germany's rule over Czechoslovakia with absolute disdain, despite the fact that she'd not been part of that country for years.

And more than one Jewish director and writer in Hollywood had fled Germany, speaking of such open discrimination that one wondered whether it could possibly be true...

She wanted to ask the dowager more questions.

The butler though cleared his throat. "Telephone for Miss Clarke."

"Me?" She'd expected it would be for the dowager, or possibly for Veronica.

She frowned. "It's not a reporter, is it?"

"It does not appear to be, Miss Clarke. If it is one, it is a most unconventional one."

Cora frowned and followed Wexley to the phone. She picked up the glossy receiver.

"Is that Cora?" An older woman's voice sounded on the other side of the crackling line.

"Yes," Cora said.

"Susan's child?"

Cora's heart squeezed. "Yes."

Was this her great aunt?

It can't be.

But the woman's accent seemed to have an Irish twang to it that made it very likely.

Very, very likely.

"Oh, my!" the woman cooed in obvious excitement. "I'm your Great Aunt Maggie."

"Hello," Cora said.

The word did not seem adequate to convey the emotion Cora felt, and Cora was glad that her great aunt could not see her rapidly warming cheeks.

"My sweet child," her great aunt said. "This makes me so very happy."

"You found me," Cora said.

"Hmph. You've gotten yourself into a mishap," Great Aunt Maggie said. "I read about it over my toast. Even managed to burn my tongue on the tea when I saw your picture. You're the spitting image of Susan."

"Really?" Cora smiled.

Her mother's current hair color was a vibrant Rita Haywoodesque red, and before that she'd had a tightly curled platinum bob à la Ginger Rogers.

Not that Mother was very likely to break out singing and dancing, like both those women were prone to doing on the silver screen.

"I didn't know that," Cora said.

"Do tell me that Susan is alive," Great Aunt Maggie said.

"She is!" Cora hastened to reassure her.

"Good," Cora's great aunt said. "Haven't heard from her in years. Now, what's all this about a murder?"

Cora shifted from foot to foot. "I suppose it sounds ridiculous."

"Perhaps. You did make all those *Gal Detective* movies." She paused. "I saw every one of them."

"You did?"

"You were excellent," Great Aunt Maggie said. "And if you really did spend the holidays snowed-in at a manor house with two murderers—"

"I did," Cora said.

"Well, then I'm very sorry. It's certainly an imperfect introduction to England."

"I'm quite fine now."

"Brave girl." Great Aunt Maggie was silent for a while, but then she said, "You should visit me in Sussex."

"Truly?"

"Sunniest part of England," Great Aunt Maggie said. "It probably doesn't compare to California, but I would like to see you."

"I'll think about it," Cora said quickly.

"Really?" The voice sounded almost surprised, but Cora repeated it again.

She was serious.

It would be nice to meet her very oldest relative.

She wasn't quite ready to go back to California yet. They chatted a while, but when she finally hung up, Wexley handed her a telegram.

"For me?" Cora raised her eyebrows, but then realized everyone in the world clearly knew her location.

Randolph took it out of the butler's hands. "Come back to Hollywood. Stop."

"Probably some joke," Cora said. "Anyone can send a telegram. I'm not going all the way back there to find—"

The phone rang again, and the butler disappeared.

He was soon back. "Miss Clarke? There is a phone call for you."

The butler gave her a curious look, as if to indicate his disapproval that she'd somehow managed to get so many messages at once.

She took the phone receiver. "Yes?"

"Darling!" A deep voice exclaimed.

"Father?" A wave of relief rushed through her.

"Merry Christmas," he said.

"M-merry Christmas," she stammered.

He'd been so disappointed in her the last time he'd seen her, but now she found herself beaming into the phone from his exuberant tone.

"Palm Springs isn't the same without you," he declared.

"Oh?"

She didn't remind him that she hadn't spent Christmas in Palm Springs since she was twelve, and even that had been accompanied with many photo shoots.

"Hello, darling!" another voice said.

"Mother?" Cora shook her head.

It couldn't be her.

Cora's mother didn't spend time with Cora's father. Not after his habit of bedding chorus girls had been discovered. Suspicions that could be ignored in private were rather less easily dismissed when they appeared splayed on the covers of gossip magazines. Her father hadn't stopped being a ladies' man when he'd slipped a ring on Mother's finger, and once his fame had risen with Cora's, he certainly hadn't halted his instincts to enjoy himself.

Still. After the trauma of the last few days, Cora was awfully glad for any contact with the outside world. Even her parents.

"Did you hear about the news?" Cora asked in a small voice.

"Naturally," her father said. "We might be thousands of miles away, but we've still got great news here."

"We want you to come back at once," Mother said.

Oh.

That was nice.

"We want you to speak to someone," Mother said.

"When I'm back?"

"Right now," Pop said.

Her father's voice seemed to beam through the receiver, and despite all the stress of the past few days, she found herself returning his smile.

"Hello, Miss Clarke."

It was Mr. Bellomo.

The head of the studio.

The man who'd dismissed her.

"Merry Christmas," Cora said.

The last time she'd seen him, he'd seemed very intent on not ever seeing her again.

"Merry Christmas to you," he repeated. "Now, I don't have time for pleasantries, we're having a smashing party here, but I am thrilled to be able to talk with you. We've got a big picture coming up, and your daddy thinks you're just the one to play opposite Pierre Ballard."

"Me?" Cora stammered. "But I don't even have a contract—"

"It's a top quality film," Mr. Bellomo continued. "We need an actress who's worldly. Someone who's seen things—" He paused. "Horrible things."

"You want me to work for you?" Cora sputtered. "Did you read the newspaper?"

She didn't want to remind him that her name was now written in big block letters on every broadsheet, but she couldn't bear for the opportunity to be taken from her once he had.

"Ah, yes. Quite the scandal you've got going," the producer said.

The thing was, his voice didn't sound appropriately upset.

"Nice way to stay in the news," he continued.

"So the offer stands?" Cora asked.

"Naturally," Mr. Bellomo said. "I don't waste time."

"Thank you for your offer."

"So we'll see you in a week," the producer said. "We'll put you in a brand new seven-year contract."

Cora hesitated. This was the call that she'd been waiting for.

She should be jumping up and down.

Her legs itched, and she wasn't certain if it was from a desire to do just that, or if she wanted to pace. Trudging on the thick snow seemed for some ridiculous reason appealing.

"I'll have to think about it," Cora said.

"Think about it?" The producer's voice became shrill. "Think?"

"Yes."

"You're not a philosopher, honey," the man said. "You're an actress. And I'm offering you work. Big work. On thousands of very large screens."

"And I'm grateful," Cora said.

"But you gotta think?" he asked resignedly.

"I'll call you," Cora said.

"Better make it soon," he said. "If you've gotta break my heart, I'd prefer to make someone else's dreams come true."

"Give me until New Year's."

"New Year's?" The man practically sputtered.

In fact, he might have sputtered, and Cora probably should have been relieved to be so far from the man's telephone.

"Yes," she said.

Cowering was in the past.

"Will that be a problem?" Cora asked.

"Of course not," he said. "This studio has many things to do while wait for you. Many, *many* things."

Cora smiled. At one point those words would have scared her. Now, she only said, "Splendid."

"Cora! Cora!" Her father's voice came through the line. It sounded frantic. "Are you still there?"

"Yes."

"Did you just tell Mr. Bellomo, Mr. Vincent Bellomo of Bellomo Studios, to wait?"

Cora smiled. "I believe I did."

"Do you know how hard it was to get him to call?"

"It's a big decision." Cora hung up the phone and went to join the others in the drawing room.

"Who was that?" Veronica asked.

"Hollywood. They—er—want me to come back. They want me to star in a new film."

Veronica beamed. "Honey, I'm so proud of you!"

"I believe they actually liked the scandal."

"How positively smashing. I'm glad this horrible holiday didn't utterly derail your career."

"I'm sorry it derailed your—"

"Marriage?" Veronica laughed, though the sound managed to be bitter. "Though that wasn't the holiday's fault. Thank goodness you found that my husband was a murderer. It's really not the sort of negative trait one can live with."

"Especially since his mistress seemed eager to leave about clues to implicate you."

"No, indeed. Though quite honestly, I do think that even divorcing in Reno is more respectable than having a partnership dissolve because of execution. I do disagree with her there."

"I don't believe she liked you," Cora said.

"No." Veronica tossed her hair. "And so many people do."

"What will you do now?"

"I'll return home. To California. And all those darling, darling fans. I'll have to see when the next ship sails for New York City. Perhaps we can spend Christmas on board. I've really no urge to spend it in this country, no matter how good mince pies are supposed to be."

Cora hesitated.

"You will be going back, won't you honey?"

It would be easy to say yes, to go along with Veronica's plan and that of her parents and Mr. Bellomo.

Everyone expected her to do that, and the decision would fulfill all her instincts for sensibleness and practicality.

But she still hesitated.

It might be nice, just this once, to do something for herself. She'd been an actress for years. These past days had taught her to not take anything for granted, even her life.

Veronica narrowed her eyes. "Honey, I do believe you don't want to come with me. You do know that I'm exciting?"

"I want to try something actually quiet."

"But you're a starlet!" Veronica said. "Quiet should not be a goal."

Cora smiled, conscious that Veronica would be just fine. Her husband might have been a murderer, an occupation that no bride would desire for her partner, but Veronica would return to Hollywood now and continue working. Cora suspected she would even enjoy it more than being an aristocrat in England, no matter if even Bel Air mansions did not equal the size of Yorkshire manor homes.

"All the same," Cora said. "I think I should try it."

"And where will you find that elusive state?" Veronica asked.

"I'll visit my great aunt in Sussex."

"On the South Downs?" Veronica rested her hand against her silk blouse and fiddled with her oversized bow in an uncharacteristic show of distress. "Heavens, you will succeed in finding quiet there. But you will be beside yourself with boredom! Why, there will be nothing to do except stare at the English Channel! And even that doesn't extend very far, nor does it have any of the magnificence of the Pacific. I doubt you'll experience a single tsunami!"

"Nevertheless, I want to visit," Cora said.

Veronica gave a languid sigh. "Very well, honey."

Cora turned to Archibald. "Do you fancy visiting Sussex?"

Archibald tilted his head to one side, as if calculating whether the strange word might entail anything delightful.

"How about a walk?" Cora asked.

At this, Archibald leaped up and dashed toward her, barking as his feet pattered against the parquet floor, and then he sprinted to the main door.

Wexley and the duchess flashed looks of disapproval, but Cora followed Archibald. She slipped his lead onto him, and they stepped outside. The ice in the moat had nearly melted, and the sky was devoid of either snow or sleet.

Archibald wagged his tail, enjoying the now-cleared drive. He marched toward the fields, away from the towering manor house and the evil that they'd found within.

ABOUT THE AUTHOR

BORN IN TEXAS, BIANCA Blythe spent four years in England. She worked in a fifteenth century castle, though sadly that didn't actually involve spotting dukes and earls strutting about in Hessians.

She credits British weather for forcing her into a library, where she discovered her first Julia Quinn novel. Thank goodness for blustery downpours.

Bianca now lives in California with her husband.

Matchmaking for Wallflowers

How to Capture a Duke

A Rogue to Avoid

Runaway Wallflower

Mad About the Baron

A Marquess for Convenience

The Wrong Heiress for Christmas

Wedding Trouble

Don't Tie the Knot

Dukes Prefer Bluestockings

The Earl's Christmas Consultant

The Sleuthing Starlet

Murder at the Manor House